Pitchers' Duel

The ball struck a small pebble and spun slowly to a stop . . .

The ball struck a small pebble and spun slowly to a stop . . .

Pitchers' Duel

A CHIP HILTON SPORTS STORY

Pitchers' Duel

BY CLAIR BEE

GROSSET & DUNLAP Publishers New York

PRINTED IN THE UNITED STATES OF AMERICA

Contents

Contents

Pitchers' Duel

Pitchers' Duel

CHAPTER 1

BLEACHER JOCKEYS

THE lower and upper frames of the scoreboard on the right-field fence showed two long rows of "goose eggs." It was the last of the eighth, one down, and the home team chucker was at bat. The tall youngster standing just outside the first-base batter's box eyed the scoreboard a second, noted the count of two and one, and then pulled his bat through in a full portside swing. Anyone who knew baseball would have caught the significance of the level bat, the smooth, flowing swing, and the last-second snap of the wrists which denotes a natural hitter.

The boy with the unsmiling gray eyes pulled his cap a little lower over his right eye and stepped into the batter's box. Oblivious to the crescendo of cheers and applause from the stands and the home team dugout, he poised the bat over his left shoulder and eyed the pitcher. The visiting chucker knew Chip Hilton; knew him to be a hard, long-ball hitter. He wasn't going to give his broad-shouldered pitching opponent anything good. He studied Hilton's wide stance and then caught the challenge of the hitter's steady gaze. That decided

1

him. He'd strike this guy out if he never pitched another game as long as he lived.

The ball came in, low and inside, and Chip let it go for a count of three and one. Stepping away from the plate, Chip's glance flickered to the third-base coaching box where Soapy Smith, cupped hands to his mouth, was talking a blue streak about "certain pitchers who couldn't find the plate."

But Soapy's right foot was kicking dirt, the sign to "take" the next pitch, and Chip sighed resignedly and stepped back into the box. He liked the "cripple" pitch, but he knew that "The Rock" was right; it was late in the game and Henry Rockwell, Valley Falls' veteran coach, was playing for one run. He wanted Chip Hilton on base, and when you were playing for Coach Rockwell you obeyed signs, or else!

Kip Parcels, Salem High School's star right-hander, wasn't going to walk Hilton if he could help it and he carefully placed a called strike right around Chip's knees for the full count. Again Chip stepped out of the box and flashed a look toward the third-base coaching box for the sign. But Soapy Smith seemed to have taken a sudden interest in Salem's left fielder. Soapy's back was toward the plate and he was hollering and making faces at his new target, and Chip knew he was "on his own."

Parcels took a slow, full windup and then put everything he had on the three-and-two pitch. The fast ball burned toward the plate waist-high. Chip's swing was perfectly timed and the meat part of his bat met the ball solidly. Chip had tagged that one, met it right on the nose, pulling a slashing Texas leaguer toward right center. His follow-through pulled him around with the hit and he dug his spikes in ever-lengthening strides as he tore along the path toward first base. Chet Stewart,

Rockwell's assistant, was standing in the first-base coaching box waving him on, and as Chip made the turn, he saw the Salem center fielder stab frantically at the bounding ball, only partially checking its flight.

The right fielder, coming over to back up the play, suddenly reversed his direction to chase the deflected ball. That was enough for the speeding base runner. Valley Falls High School state champions needed the run he carried and they would have a good chance to get it if Chip Hilton could reach third. Chip really turned on the steam then, rounding second without breaking stride and heading for the Salem third sacker, who was straddling the bag with hands outstretched toward the throw from right field. Chip knew it was going to be close.

Soapy Smith was down on his knees in the third-base coaching box, arms extended toward the bag with palms down, screaming, *"Hit the dirt, Chip! Hit the dirt!"*

Twelve feet from the bag, Chip took off in a headlong belly dive, arms reaching desperately for the bag. His hands met the sack a split second before the third sacker dug the gloved ball viciously into his back. Chip got to one knee, holding his breath, afraid to look at the base umpire. Then an explosive roar from the home stands greeted the decision and Chip knew he was safe. He scrambled to his feet, brushing the dirt from his uniform with his cap, happy in the knowledge that he had set up the run the Big Reds needed so badly. He flashed a quick smile at Soapy and glanced toward the dugout. Coach Rockwell caught the glance and shook his fist in Chip's direction.

"Atta boy, Chipper! Atta boy!"

Everyone in the park knew the play now. The Big Reds' coach would squeeze this run in now, for sure! And in spite of Parcels and his clever pitching, that's exactly what Rockwell did. After a huddle out at the mound in which the Salem coach talked earnestly to Parcels, the Salem infield moved in with the obvious intention of cutting off the run at the plate.

Parcels pitched them high and low to Tuffy Collins, with Chip breaking toward the plate with every throw and back to third when the ball thudded into the catcher's glove. Then, on the three-and-no pitch, Collins met a low pitch and dumped a perfect bunt down the third-base line. Chip was "in" for the first run of the game almost as soon as Parcels had fielded the ball, sliding headlong under and through the catcher who was trying to block the plate. The Salem chucker didn't even try for the play at the plate and his hard throw barely nipped a speeding Tuffy at first for the second out. Then Speed Morris, the Big Reds' flashy shortstop, hit the first pitch straight to the Salem first sacker for the third out and the Big Reds scrambled out of the dugout for the top of the ninth, out in front by a run.

Chip walked slowly out toward the mound, stopping on the way to pick up his glove. Then he heard them again, heard them riding the Rock. The loud, raucous voices were bitter, persistent, and familiar.

"You're just plain lucky, cement head!"

"Rockwell, why don't you quit while your luck's good?"

"Yeah, grandpa, you're two years past the retirement age right now! Why don't ya give some young guy a chance?"

"You're a has-been, Rockwell! Just a has-been!"

Chip stopped in his tracks and turned to look at the six or seven young men who had been razzing and taunting Rockwell all through the game. He knew each one well, knew each to be exactly what he was trying to brand Rockwell.

"Hey, look at Rockwell's pet! He's *mad* at us!"

"What *you* lookin' at, Hilton? Go on out there on the hill and quit grandstanding. We'll be rid of you, too, in another three weeks!"

"Yeah, grandstander, don't look so tough. Your mother won't like it!"

"No, nor grandpappy Rockwell, either!"

"Two of a kind, you two—you and Rockwell, Hilton!"

"Yeah, two fools for luck!"

The crowd in the stands had taken sides now, a few joining the hecklers in attacking Rockwell and Hilton, while the majority showed their displeasure with the poor sportsmanship of the loud-voiced group. The whole field was in an uproar.

Carl Carey walked out from behind the plate thumping the ball in his catcher's glove as Speed Morris, Chuck Badger, Tuffy Collins, and Biggie Cohen came trotting up to join Chip. Cohen grasped Hilton by the arm. "Come on, Chip, we'll take care of them later. Let's win the game!"

"Yeah, Chip, don't let 'em get your goat!"

The roar grew louder as Rockwell leaped from the dugout and walked quickly toward the group of players on the base line. "Forget it, Chip," he said quietly. "Finish the game. That's all that matters." He gestured toward the stands. "They mean nothing—"

Rockwell grasped Chip by both arms and firmly eased him around to face the diamond. Then he slapped the tall youngster gently on the back and gave him a little push toward the pitcher's mound.

"Play ball! Play ball! Play ball!"

The plate umpire, mask in hand, broke up the little group of players, and the mood of the crowd changed almost instantly. "Play ball," came booming from the stands, "play ball!"

Chip was seething as he took his warm-up pitches. This had been going on all spring. Game after game, at home or away, this same group of hecklers had plagued Rockwell and the team until it had become almost unbearable.

Directly behind the plate, in the grandstand, a small bronze-faced man sat quietly listening to the yells, cheers, catcalls, and general crowd-conversation during the commotion. Now he concentrated once again upon the lanky, blond kid out on the mound. He heard what was being said, but he was chiefly concerned with the young chucker's reaction to the crowd-baiting.

"Don't know why they're riding Hilton," someone said. "He's won every game he's pitched!"

"Yeah, and leading the team in hitting, too!"

"Best pitcher in the state!" a booming voice asserted.

"Ready for the big leagues right now!" someone added.

The bronze-faced man turned to the fan seated next to him. "Those fellers with the other team?" he asked, nodding toward the noisy group who had been riding Rockwell.

"Them?" his seatmate asked, glancing at the hecklers. "No, no—they're from Valley Falls, all right—but they hate Rockwell! He's the coach, you know." He nodded toward the loud-mouthed fans again. "Those fellows have been after Rockwell for two years. Want him to quit so they can get one of their own crowd up at the school as the coach."

"That's funny," the stranger said dryly, "the guy gives them a state championship team in three sports and they want him ditched! Don't get it!"

"Well, it's a long story. Rock's sorta independent and runs his own job. Some of those back-alley alumni wanted to mastermind the teams and the old boy wouldn't hold still for it. Don't blame him! Anyway, they resent the way the coach ignores 'em and now it's a regular feud—

"That fellow with the red face is Jerry Davis. Son of old man Davis who runs the big jewelry store in town. Wise guy, the kid! Big-mouthed and sorta flashy—

"Frank Waters and Dick Cantwell, sitting next to him, aren't such bad guys, but they run around with Davis and he's got them under his thumb. They do just about what Jerry wants them to do.

"The two tough-looking geezers on the end are Buck Adams and Peck Weaver. Town toughs and always in hot water about something."

Further conversation ceased as the first hitter of the big end of the Salem batting order tapped the plate with his bat and the slender youngster on the mound toed the rubber. Chip was still burning with anger, but it wasn't apparent in his pitching. He mowed the Salem hitters down in one-two-three order, turned abruptly about as he delivered the last strike, and headed for Ohlsen Stadium and the dressing room in the high school building just beyond. Trooping after him came his teammates and little Paddy Jackson, the bat boy, trotting along with Chip's warm-up jacket.

Bringing up the rear, the two game umpires walked slowly along talking about the game and Coach Henry Rockwell.

"Old guy sure stands up, doesn't he?"

"Rock? Sure! Just as much fight as ever!"

His companion laughed. "You can say that again! Hasn't changed in the last twenty years, far as I can see!"

"That gang of roughnecks sure worked him over. I didn't like it!"

"Me neither. For fifty cents I'd have had them tossed

out of the stand. Hear they're trying to force the school
board to retire him!"

"Force is right! He won't quit! Ain't built that way!"

"State law says all teachers must be retired at sixty-
three and Rock's way past that, I guess. They could take
it to court and force him out."

"Probably the only way they could do it! Rock's sore
and he'll fight tooth and toenail!"

The last person to leave the grandstand was the
bronze-faced stranger. He made his way leisurely along
the wide wooden grandstand seat and down the broad
steps to the concrete walk leading to the street. He had
enjoyed the game he had just witnessed for several reasons. The number one reason was the sensational all-
around play of a young high school chucker by the
name of William "Chip" Hilton. The tall, slender tow-
head was three weeks away from graduation and Stu
Gardner might have been his shadow, the way he followed every move the boy made.

The other reason for Gardner's enjoyment of the
game was another Valley Falls High School senior who
knew just how to play first base. Biggie Cohen was six
feet two or three, left-handed, and possessed of a strong
arm. Fast of foot and hand, the big boy was a master of
the shift and the stretch, as well as the pickup. The
bulky youngster was an ideal first sacker. Gardner had
worried a bit about the two hundred and thirty pounds
Cohen carried until he had checked the kid's physical
make-up. Then he had ceased to give that further
thought; Cohen was as strong as a bull and there wasn't
an ounce of fat on his body. The agile first sacker was a
good competitor, too. He hit the long ball, and Stu
had him tabbed as a sure-fire, big-league prospect.

Stewart Gardner had been in organized baseball a
long time, first as a player, later as manager of a Triple

A class club, and now as a scout for a big-league chain. It was his job to discover talent, weigh it carefully, and sign it up as economically as possible if he felt it justified his boss's rigid requirements. Stu Gardner had been watching the Valley Falls Big Reds for the past month and he had canceled all thoughts of his other prospects for the time being. Right here in Valley Falls he had discovered two athletes who would make his job secure for years to come if they were as good as they had looked in the past few games. *And* if he could get them to sign a contract.

Gardner was a thorough individual, painstaking in his personal life and in his work. In his scouting, he charted each prospect's emotional stability as thoroughly as his physical ability. The veteran scout was certain both youngsters possessed plenty of baseball ability, but emotional balance was something you couldn't spot from the grandstand; you really had to know a kid to judge him on that score. Stu decided to concentrate on that important end of his job at the first opportunity. He had been a little disturbed by Hilton's reaction to the razzing because he had known a lot of fine ballplayers who might have enjoyed a successful big-league career had they possessed self-control.

A big-league scout isn't paid just to travel around the country watching games and players; he's got to deliver, got to turn up a real ballplayer every so often. Stu Gardner was past due, way past due. Now, as he sauntered along behind the crowd, he breathed a fervent prayer that the kids he had been watching would not be found wanting in mental discipline, and that he would be the only big-league scout to see Chip Hilton and Biggie Cohen play baseball before graduation, only three weeks away, ended their high school careers and made them eligible to sign a big-league contract.

CHAPTER 2

DIAMOND POLITICS

CHIP HILTON hadn't spoken a word since he had pivoted and started for the dressing room after the third strike on the last Salem batter. Leaning back against his locker, relaxing from that after-game tiredness which always hits a fellow so suddenly, he tried to get the anger out of his heart. The riding he had taken today was just about the last straw. A fellow could take just so much. . . .

The Big Reds' small squad was composed of two groups. One from the South Side and one from the West Side. The West Side was represented by most of the members of what was jokingly and familiarly known as the Hilton Athletic Club. The Hilton home was the "club's" quarters; the members were Chip's closest friends, and most of them were on the Valley Falls varsity squad. They included Speed Morris, shortstop; Biggie Cohen, first base; Soapy Smith, catcher, pitcher, and outfielder; and Red Schwartz, outfielder.

The South Side representatives were Chuck Badger, stocky, heavy-set third baseman; Nick Trullo, husky southpaw; Carl Carey, a fighting catcher who shared the receiving with Soapy Smith; and Tuffy Collins, peppery second baseman and chief "holler" player on the team.

These two groups, former rivals, had been brought close together by several incidents in which Chip Hilton figured prominently. Then, appreciating the athletic potentialities of the two groups, Rockwell had cleverly substituted team spirit for neighborhood competition. While engaged in this pursuit he had gained the respect and loyalty of both groups. Now the cowardly attacks by Rockwell's enemies had welded the team into a fighting squad, each youngster willing and eager to play his heart out in his desire to help his coach.

Every sports fan in town knew that Rockwell's enemies had been waging a relentless campaign to force the veteran mentor to accept retirement. And a few of these realized that retirement meant the end of the one thing in the world that the veteran coach liked best to do: coach athletics and boys. But every ballplayer on Valley Falls' state championship team knew how Rockwell felt, and every one of them wished he could do something about it.

Rockwell and his assistant, Chet Stewart, had remained behind to help gather up the ball bag, the bats, and the bases, and to help Taps Browning, the manager, carry the usual assortment of water pails, first-aid bags, and other equipment to the gym. After a last checkup to see that nothing had been overlooked, the two coaches and the manager trudged slowly along behind the umpires, and were the last to reach the locker room.

Rockwell's stocky figure was clothed in an old, faded tight-fitting baseball suit which seemed molded to his body. The clack-clack, clackety-clack of his spikes rang out sharply and warned the Big Reds of his approach, but they didn't look up when he came clattering into the locker room. Just inside the door, Rockwell paused and his eyes swept the room from one boy to another. He sensed that the kids were full of bitterness over the riding to which he and Chip had been subjected and he decided right then and there to get the resentment out of their heads. The quicker the better!

This team stood in grave danger of coming apart at the seams. Not because of conditioning, injuries, or lack of ability, but because of emotional stress. He had seen it coming ever since Davis and the South Side roughnecks had started their riding campaign at the very first game. He'd fix that! Right now! He'd get their minds off that problem! He'd do a little riding himself!

Rockwell had a good weapon. The annual elections were to be held shortly to choose members of the senior class to take over a one-day administration of the municipal government of Valley Falls. The ball club members had talked of little else during the past two weeks.

The Big Reds knew Rockwell's moods and his first words warned them that he was angry. "That was a fine exhibition," he stormed. "You fellows must have been reading last year's press clippings! You're sure not playing like last year's ball club!

"If it isn't asking too much, I'd like to request more concentration on defending the state baseball championship, and less on the school political campaigns!"

Rockwell's sharp black eyes darted from one boy to another. The kids were startled. Good! He had them going! . . .

"Another thing," he snapped, "I don't want to hear any more talk about being stale!" He paused to let that sink in and then continued, biting off his words sharply. "You have to be good to go stale! Now beat it! And show up here tomorrow thinking baseball, playing baseball, and looking like baseball players—not like Third Ward politicians! That's all!"

A little later Chip, Soapy Smith, Biggie Cohen, Red Schwartz and Taps Browning piled into Speed Morris' red-and-white jalopy and started for home. This evening, there was an absence of the usual bickering, cat-calling, and needling. Everyone seemed subdued except Soapy Smith. He leaned forward and tapped Speed Morris on the shoulder.

"This crate's on its last legs, my friend," he said warningly. "You ever hear about the one-horse shay?"

"Yeah, we heard about it," Biggie said menacingly, "but you better forget about it—"

Then, just as Soapy had predicted, the tired old jalopy burped, chuckled a few times as if anticipating coming events, and stopped dead.

"You and your big mouth," Biggie growled, "why don't you keep it shut?"

Soapy nodded grimly. "Yeah," he agreed, "why don't I?"

Speed raised the battered hood. "Looks just the same," he said dryly.

"Yeah," Soapy agreed, "just the same as it did thirty years ago! Well, Speed, you're supposed to be a mechanic. Show us how good you are. Hah! This I gotta see!"

For the next fifteen minutes Soapy was quiet, even though he was clever enough to avoid a couple of turns on the small end of the crank. Then he could stand it no longer.

"It's tired," he said wearily, "tired like me. Well," he gasped, "we gotta get someone to shove us over the hill."

"Fat chance," Schwartz grunted. "Who'd risk a bumper on this thing! C'mon gang," he said. "Come on, let's shove. If we can make it to the top of the hill, we'll be okay."

Digging in, they puffed and pushed, but the jalopy made little progress up the steep grade. Soapy pushed, too, but he kept a weather eye over his shoulder. And a car did come along, a car with a big "SHERIFF" painted on the side.

"It's Sheriff Birks's car and Early's driving," Soapy yelled hopefully. "Hey, Early, give us a shove, will ya?"

The black car slowed down and young Early Birks leaned out to get a better view of the proceedings. "What goes?" he yelled, grinning delightedly. "Havin' trouble, fellas? Looks like good exercise! See you tomorrow! Take it easy, Soapy!" The car shot forward and up over the hill, but a derisive, "Heyuh, heyuh, heyuh," echoed back in its wake.

"Well, whaddaya know about that," Soapy managed. "Whaddaya know!"

"I know you oughtta kept your big mouth shut," Biggie growled. "What's the matter with you—laying us open for a guy like that? Why ask him?"

"Who wants to shove?"

"I'd rather shove than ask a favor of Early Birks."

"Whaddaya mean favor?" Soapy demanded. "It's a town car, ain't it? We got as much right to use that car as Early has, ain't we? Town cars are s'ported by taxes, ain't they? And our old dads pay the freight, don't they? Heck, we got more right to use that car than Early Birks has!"

"How you figure that?" Speed demanded.

Soapy grunted. "Easy! There's more of us!"

Schwartz laughed. "Get a long way in this town with that philosophy," he said. "Two feet—maybe."

"Yeah, why not?" Soapy demanded. "You tell my why not?"

Speed laughed. "Because Mayor Condon and Boiler

Cowles and Sheriff Birks have this town locked up," he said. "That's why!"

Soapy was belligerent. "Whaddaya mean, locked up?"

"You know what he means," Schwartz said sourly. "He means those three guys run the town! Anything they want to do—they do!"

"Why don't we throw 'em out?" Soapy persisted. "Answer me that! Maybe we could, if we could vote!" he beamed. "Soon as we can vote, we'll throw 'em out!"

"Take more than a few votes to throw them out," Biggie said slowly. "They're organized! You know," he continued softly, "I like that Early less and less every day. He and his pals are trying to run things at school just like his old man and his crowd run the town. Take the school municipal elections—Early's running for sheriff and Ralph Cowles wants to be the chief of police."

"Right!" Soapy interrupted. "And Mark Condon wants to keep the mayor stuff in the family! And you know what? He'll do it!"

"He won't if I can do anything about it," Biggie drawled. "Maybe we oughtta draw up a platform and elect some regular guys—"

"Hey," Soapy shouted, "I've got an idea. Let's put Chip up for mayor. He'll win in a walk!"

Red Schwartz was enthusiastic. "Atta baby, Soapy," he cried. "It's a cinch! Whaddaya say, Chip?"

"No, thanks," Chip said firmly. "I've got enough headaches now. We've got enough to do to defend the state championship," he said quietly. "Look, we don't want to get mixed up in that municipal election stuff. We've got plenty to do playing ball. Remember what Rock said. Let's skip it!"

"I sure hate to see that crowd get in," Schwartz

grumbled. "Socks, they run the student council and the student court and everything else. You know what'll happen just as well as I do! Young Mark Condon will head up the Citizens' ticket and run for mayor, and Ralph Cowles will run for chief of police, and Early Birks will be the candidate for sheriff; and the rest of their crowd will be appointed to the town council. Aw, heck, I can see 'em right now!"

"Not if Chip will run," Speed said. "Chip would win easy!"

"Right," Soapy added. "You run, Chip, and I bet you a million bucks you win!"

"It's too bad Mayor Stanton and Sheriff Brock lost the town election last year," Speed said resignedly.

"Well, the people elected them," Schwartz said. "They asked for it!"

"Unhuh," Biggie grunted, "and they got Condon and Birks."

"They got more than that," Schwartz added. "They got old man Davis, Cantwell, and Frank Greer on the council, and Boiler Cowles for chief of police."

"There're some good men on the Board," Chip said. "J. P. Ohlsen's a member, and Mr. Stanton—and George Thomas."

"If they're so good," Soapy objected, "why don't they do something about Condon and Cowles and Birks and the rest of them—"

"Because they don't have a majority," Biggie explained patiently. "Don't you understand? There's only two or three good men on the council. The others, the majority, are all Condon's pals."

Red Schwartz had the floor now and he really opened up. "Wonder if Ohlsen and Stanton and Thomas know about all the fishing trips in the town cars, and the protection Adams and Weaver get from Cowles for their gambling house over on the South Side, and the new walk the city engineer built up to Mayor Condon's house. And— Aw, what's the use!"

Speed took over. "How about all the materials? Who paid for them?" he demanded.

"You can bet Condon didn't!" Biggie said dryly.

"You know," Soapy gravely informed his friends, "my old man's always raving about the high tax rate and I'm beginning to see the light!"

"You'll see a light, all right," Biggie rumbled, "and hear a little bell tinkling, too, if you ask any more favors from Early Birks."

Soapy started to say something, but catching the glint in Biggie's eyes he bustled around back of the car and cautiously applied his shoulder to a rear fender. "C'mon guys," he said, "let's go. I gotta be to work at seven o'clock."

While the charter members of the Hilton A. C. were having jalopy trouble, Jerry Davis, Frank Waters, and Dick Cantwell were rolling along in the Davis' family Cadillac.

"You gotta hand it to that kid," Waters said grudgingly, "he's got it!"

Jerry Davis nodded. "He's good all right, if you like his kind."

"Boy, he was sore today," Cantwell chuckled. "I thought for a minute he was coming right up into the stands."

Davis grinned. "Weaver and Adams sure had him going. They hate his guts!"

"Why shouldn't they," Waters asked dryly. "Didn't he lick Peck over on the hill last year, right in front of the whole South Side? Sure they hate his guts!"

"Hold everything," Davis said softly. "I've got an idea. A good idea!"

"What?" Waters asked.

"Something good! You know how Zimmerman won't tolerate fighting? Well, why not maneuver Hilton into a fight with Adams or Weaver at one of the games?"

"So what?"

"So what? Nothing much, 'cept Zimmerman will suspend Hilton and we'll have Rockwell right where we want him! Get it?"

"No."

Davis made a gesture of exasperation. "Trullo's the only other pitcher, isn't he? And you know how Rockwell is—he won't use a kid more than every four days. That'll leave only *one* chucker!"

"I get it! Then they'll start to lose—"

"Right! And since everyone in town thinks the team's a cinch to repeat with the championship—"

"You mean they'll blame Rockwell?"

"You know how folks in this town are. They can't stand to lose. And sure as shooting they'll put pressure on the school board and we'll be rid of the old goat for good!"

CHAPTER 3

BLUE LAWS

VALLEY FALLS High School normally would have been buzzing about yesterday's victory and the pitching duel between Kip Parcels and Chip Hilton. But not this Friday morning. Between classes and in every corridor, hall, and classroom, politicians waxed briefly eloquent as they promoted their various candidates for the senior elections. At lunchtime, the broad stone steps leading to the main entrance and the gymnasium terrace in the rear were thronged with students discussing the party platforms and the possible candidates.

That afternoon Principal Zimmerman called a special meeting in the main auditorium where the entire student body assembled. The ball club, bored by the whole affair, sat together in one long row.

Mayor Condon and several members of the town council were seated on the stage and, after the orchestra completed a short musical program, each councilman spoke briefly. Principal Zimmerman then extolled the virtues of "our great mayor," and Condon was presented. The town's top executive greeted the students warmly and advised them that he and his entire administration were looking forward to Friday, June 18th,

19

when the town government would be turned over for the day to the successful student electees. He promised the full co-operation of each city administrator and stated that every office would be prepared for the "invasion."

Mayor Condon was a bit patronizing and inclined to be humorous as he spoke of the enthusiasm with which the members of the city government were "fashioning keys to the city for their successors on Friday, June 18th."

While Mayor Condon was talking, Chip absent-mindedly was reading a little blue law clipping which had been printed in the *Yellow Jacket*. It read: "*In Kansas City, Missouri, only married women and girls over seventeen can wear lipstick.*"

Chip smiled at a sudden thought. "A fellow could have lots of fun if he got elected and then enforced all the old blue laws. Hey," he muttered to himself, "*there* was an idea!" Then Chip had a more serious thought. Why, a fellow could do some real things on Friday, June 18th, if the mayor was sincere in what he said and a fellow had the right crowd behind him.

As he thought over the matter, the germ of an idea began to develop in his mind. Why, maybe a guy could even square up some personal debts. He sighed. Better skip it . . . Better concentrate on the baseball . . . He probably wouldn't be elected even if he became a candidate. . . .

But in spite of himself, his thoughts jumped back to the previous evening in the Sugar Bowl. Chip's friends had again urged him to let them nominate him for mayor.

"Aw, c'mon, Chip," Soapy had pleaded. "You'd win in a walk. You could be the mayor and Biggie could be the chief of police, an', an'—I—I could be the city auditor.

I'd like to be the auditor and count all the money and find out where it's all goin'. Whaddaya say? Nobody likes those guys. They just elect them 'cause nobody else runs. Whaddaya say?"

But Chip was adamant in his decision to concentrate on baseball; he had told them he didn't have time, not with school and work and baseball.

Speed, Biggie, Red, and Taps Browning had joined Soapy in pressuring Chip, but to no avail. Petey Jackson got his oar in, too, and just about summarized everyone's arguments when he said, "Aw, c'mon, have some fun. All you do is work all the time—you're too serious!"

But Chip had stuck to his guns and his companions had finally given up. Now, for a brief moment, Chip was sorry he had been so determined. It could have been fun. . . .

Just before the end of the assembly, Principal Zimmerman announced that the Home Rule party nominations would be held at the three o'clock assembly, June 2nd, and the Citizens party nominations on the following day, Thursday, June 3rd, at two o'clock. The elections would be held on Wednesday, June 9th, with the polls open from one o'clock to three o'clock in the gymnasium. He promised that the results would be announced late that afternoon before the end of the Parkton game.

Rockwell liked his ballplayers to be able to play more than one position. And one of his favorite deals was to insist that his catchers and pitchers shag flies as a conditioner. This year, practice with respect to his chuckers and receivers was extremely important because it was necessary for him to use one of his batteries in the outfield every game.

Coach Henry Rockwell had been handicapped the

year before with a small squad, but had nursed the team through to win the state championship. But that feat had been nothing compared to the task facing him this year. His outfield was patrolled by only one regular— Red Schwartz, in center field. And since no new candidate had shown up, Rockwell had been forced to use one of his catchers, Carl Carey or Soapy Smith, and one of his pitchers, Chip Hilton or Nick Trullo, in the other outfield spots.

The only other player available was little Lefty Peters who had been used as a pitcher the year before until stricken with an appendicitis attack, which required an emergency operation. Lefty was back, but had never fully recovered, and Rockwell had never used him on the hill and only once or twice in the outfield.

Chip Hilton was a ballplayer's ballplayer, a hard, consistent hitter, who could pull in flies, throw with the best of them, and who fielded his pitching position flawlessly. But there Rockwell's good luck ended. Soapy Smith and Nick Trullo were both equipped with strong throwing arms, but were uncertain fielders. Carl Carey and Lefty Peters seemed unable to judge fly balls and neither possessed throwing arms sufficiently strong to handle the long throws, particularly from right field to third base.

Rockwell assigned Friday afternoon's infield practice to his assistant, Chet Stewart, and personally spent the whole practice session with the outfield. Time after time he lifted high flies, long, low drives, and an occasional hard grasscutter to Chip, Lefty Peters, Nick Trullo, Carl Carey, Soapy Smith, and Red Schwartz. After two hours of this grinding practice, Rockwell grunted and sent them on three laps around the field and to the showers.

Petey Jackson, Valley Falls' leading soda jerk, was taking advantage of the late afternoon business lull to read a copy of the high school paper, the *Yellow Jacket*. Petey had dropped out of high school some years before, but he was still interested in anything that concerned the Big Reds and Valley Falls High School. Chip Hilton was one of Petey's heroes and the two boys had worked at the Sugar Bowl for several years. The previous summer Soapy Smith had been added to the staff and the three youngsters made up a happy working combination for John Schroeder's Sugar Bowl.

Petey read the *Yellow Jacket* aloud, mumbling the words faster and faster as he read about the coming elections and the possible candidates. "Same old crowd," he muttered, "same old crowd. Trying to run everything —Early Birks, Ralph Cowles, Mark Condon, and that bunch—" Petey snorted and threw the paper over his shoulder. Then he picked up the afternoon edition of the *Times*. Turning to the sports page, he focused his attention on the *Times and Sports*. "He's at it again," Petey mumbled, halfway through the column. "What's the matter with that guy!"

TIMES AND SPORTS

By Muddy Waters

Valley Falls High School may be the defending diamond champions of the state, but it is this writer's humble opinion that the Big Reds will watch the current year's championship games at State on June 23, 25, and 26 from the bleachers . . .

Because Rockwell has but two hurlers and both are overworked . . . Because prima donna Chip Hilton makes with the temperament and can't take a little bleacher riding . . . Because the Big Reds have won or lost every game so far by a single run.

Because Biggie Cohen is the only regular hitting consistently . . . Because sixteen runs and twenty-nine hits in

seven games against the weakest teams in Section Two indi-
cate an absence of power . . . Because Henry Rockwell
has overtrained the squad and is trying to teach high school
kids big-league baseball. . . .

Petey couldn't take any more. He slammed the paper
down on the marble top of the soda fountain and loudly
expressed his opinion of a certain sports columnist. And
right then and there he decided that come tomorrow
afternoon his grandmother was going to be dangerously
ill and he personally was going to check up on the Big
Reds' baseball team.

Petey figured he'd need full co-operation from his
grandmother, for Saturday afternoons were busy afternoons and John Schroeder might take a notion to check
up. So that night Petey hurried right past the poolroom,
having invested his pleasure money in a nice box of
candy.

The next morning John Schroeder was unusually kind
when Petey referred to his grandmother's sudden ill-
ness. "Of course," he insisted, when Petey demurred
feebly. "Of course you're going home! We'll make out!
Everybody will be at the game, anyway!"

Chip and Soapy were deeply concerned about Petey's
grandmother, too. They knew her well.

"What's the matter with her?" Chip asked.

Petey sighed heavily. "It's spells she gets, Chip. They
just come—sudden-like, of course—"

"What kind of spells?" Soapy asked solicitously.

"Well, it's a kind of a sugar spell," Petey explained
uncertainly. "You've heard of that?"

Soapy nodded. "Oh, sure! I know about that—"

"Is there anything we can do?" Chip asked anxiously.

"No," Petey said sadly, "there's nothing much anyone
can do. She'll snap out of it tomorrow."

"We'll stop by and see her," Soapy said consolingly, "on our way to the game."

"Oh, no," Petey cried hastily, "don't do that. You'll upset her!"

"You sure?"

Petey was sure, and at twelve o'clock he hurried home to make sure about that and to figure out another problem which had just come to mind.

John Schroeder and Doc Jones were rabid sports fans. Ranking high in Valley Falls' roster of solid and respected citizens, the two cronies were strong believers in the value of high school athletics. And when Henry Rockwell's Big Reds played a game, any kind of game, these two were sure to be on hand.

Like most small towns, Saturday afternoon was Valley Falls' business day of the week. Granting that his patients' shopping problems encouraged Doc Jones to eliminate office hours on Saturday afternoons, it was difficult to understand why John Schroeder should not be on the job at his drugstore and the Sugar Bowl. That is, of course, unless you knew John Schroeder, knew that he was financially secure, that business—like athletics—was a hobby, and that he was keenly interested in the sports achievements of one of his employees.

Chip Hilton had worked in John Schroeder's Sugar Bowl for several years. Schroeder was extremely fond of the boy and had arranged Chip's working hours so they would not interfere with his schoolwork nor participation in athletics. Chip was extremely grateful for John Schroeder's kindness and he had earned his employer's deepest respect because he never shirked his responsibilities.

Compared to the bleachers, baseball's grandstand seats fill slowly. But if all grandstand fans were as rabid as John Schroeder and Doc Jones, the reverse would have been true. These two Big Red rooters liked to watch the pre-game hitting, fielding, and warm-up practice almost as much as the game. This afternoon they were the first grandstand customers to arrive and gleefully hurried to their favorite seats, right behind the plate and high up in the grandstand.

"What a day, what a day," Doc gasped enthusiastically, as he puffed along behind John Schroeder. "Makes a man feel almost like living."

The doctor was correct in his meteorologic observation. It was perfect baseball weather, late spring with just a hint of the hot summer days to come in the soft, warm breeze.

The Big Reds had finished their hitting practice. Now the sharp crack of Delford's bats resounded in the tight little park and brought scattered cheers from the bleachers back of the visitors' dugout. The bleachers extended out from the small grandstand parallel with the foul lines. And both sides were fairly well filled. Here and there a white shirt stood out in the crowd, attesting to the warmth of the sun's rays.

John Schroeder and Doc Jones were the first grandstand customers, all right, but the first bleacherites to arrive were Buck Adams, Peck Weaver, and three or four of their followers. This crew had arrived early and were seated in the front row of the bleachers right on the first-base side of the field and right above the Valley Falls dugout. And they were unusually quiet.

Chip, leisurely limbering up with Carl Carey in front of the dugout, gave no sign that he noted the presence of the hecklers, but he was puzzled. Too good to be true, he mused. They're up to something.

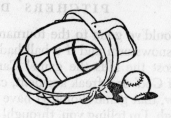

CHAPTER 4

CANDIDATE FOR MAYOR

TRULLO started for the Big Reds with Soapy Smith behind the plate. And while the big southpaw was warming up, someone right behind the dugout started an argument with another bleacherite. Chip, almost at their feet under the shelter of the dugout roof, could hear the hecklers as clearly as if he had been right smack in their midst. Rockwell, he noted with a quick side glance, seemed completely oblivious to the heated conversation.

"Rockwell's all washed up! Hasn't kept up with the times!"

"Times or no times, he keeps winning—"

"How you figure that? Look what happened last fall in football! Had a veteran squad! Same team that won the state championship the year before! How about that?"

"Yes, but he was sick! Wasn't with the team part of the season. They finished strong when he got back! Knocked off Steeltown, the state champs! Is that bad?"

"How about basketball? Didn't lose a man from the team that won the championship the year before! How d'ya explain that?"

"Would've gone to the tournament if it hadn't been for a snowstorm and if a ball hadn't deflated in the air and cost the kids the game! Can't blame him for an 'act of God' or a freak accident, can you?"

"Aw, that game shouldn't have even been close. He's through, I'm telling you, through! Look, you don't mean to say that you approve of him keeping some up-and-coming young coach out of a job, do you?"

"Well, maybe I do and maybe I don't. Can't see as how that's got anything to do with coaching, though—"

A sudden burst of cheers from the Delford bleachers and an answering roar from the Big Reds' rooters drowned out the argument. The game was on.

Like many lefties, Nick Trullo was wild and fast. That combination smothers most hitters. But Delford waited him out and it paid off. Nick walked the first three batters, struck out the cleanup man, and then walked in the first run of the game. Before the side was retired, Delford had scored three runs.

Trullo's wildness seemed to affect his teammates; they could do nothing right. At bat, they hit straight at the fielders for easy outs and, in the field, nothing clicked. In the bottom half of the seventh, with the Big Reds trailing 8 to 0, and the home fans on their feet for the stretch, Weaver and Adams suddenly came to life with a vicious attack upon Rockwell. But most of it was lost in the crowd tumult.

Rockwell and Stewart and Pop, the trainer, and little Paddy, Chip, Carl Carey, and all the Big Reds were out in front of the dugout pleading with Tuffy Collins to "start the fire" and for the Big Reds to "go get some runs!"

Tuffy pounded the plate with his bat and, just as Rockwell started down the dugout steps, Peck Weaver leaned over the low roof and dashed a paper cup and its contents right in the face of the unsuspecting coach. The thing was done so quickly and so cleverly that it was seen by few, if any, spectators.

Chip was close behind Rockwell and some of the liquid splattered into his eyes. But he had seen Weaver commit the act and, without thinking, he dashed around the dugout, vaulted the low railing, and was on top of Weaver, swinging away, almost before anyone else could move. Anyone else, that is, except a slender, bearded man wearing a hat with its brim turned down all around his face. The stranger moved with unusual speed as he joined Chip in the battle. Although several people recalled the affair later and wondered who the man could be, it was no mystery to two persons who had a good view of the incident from their vantage point high in the grandstand.

Soapy Smith, Carl Carey, Speed Morris, and Biggie Cohen were right behind the bearded stranger, over the rail and into the melee, and in no time at all, Peck Weaver, Buck Adams, and sundry other members of the gang were absorbing a thorough going over. It took the combined efforts of Rockwell, Chet Stewart, Principal Zimmerman, and the only officer of the law who was present, big Bob Gilbert, to get the thoroughly enraged players back down on the field again.

All over the park, in the bleachers, and in the grandstand, the fans were standing on tiptoe trying to get a good view of the proceedings.

"What happened?"

"Who they after?"

"Who's fighting?"

"Looks like someone started something they couldn't finish!"

Chip followed his teammates back on the field, still boiling, but feeling a bit of satisfaction because he had given Peck Weaver a good trimming. But he wasn't prepared for the descent from the stands of the Valley Falls High School principal. The school prexy made straight for Chip, anger written all over his face.

"That was a disgraceful exhibition, Hilton," he said heatedly, "you may consider yourself suspended from baseball and from Valley Falls High School as of this minute! Leave the field immediately and see me in my office Tuesday at eleven o'clock." Zimmerman turned on his heel and returned to the grandstand.

"But, Zim," Rockwell remonstrated, following along behind the principal, "we're playing Stratford Monday, and Chip's got to work that game—"

Zimmerman's blue eyes were hard and unyielding as he faced Rockwell. "Hilton is suspended, Hank," he said firmly, "from baseball and from school." He turned away and again started for the stands.

Rockwell kept pace with the irate school administrator, talking earnestly. "They started it, Zim, it wasn't Chip's fault—"

Zimmerman paused once more. "I saw the whole thing, Hank. A player should be able to take a little good-natured joshing from the spectators. Hilton lost his head. A captain is supposed to set a good example for his team. I won't discuss it further until Tuesday."

"Good-natured joshing?" Rockwell fumed. "If that's your idea of fun, one of us is out of his mind!"

But Rockwell was talking to himself and the empty air.

And he was talking to himself two innings later as he trudged past the scoreboard with his arms full of baseball equipment. "Whitewashed," he muttered, "whitewashed eleven to nothing! And who's going to work Monday? This could ruin our whole season!"

The local rooters were low in spirits as they made their way out of the stands. All except John Schroeder and Doc Jones. They attracted considerable crowd displeasure by bursting into long laughter from time to time. However, as soon as they noted the shocked expressions on the faces of near-by fans, they subsided into low chuckles and subdued tones.

"When did you first recognize Petey?" Jones asked.

Schroeder chuckled again. "Oh, long before the game started. Of course, when he went to Chip's aid there was no doubt about it."

Doc Jones wiped a tear from his eye. "I can still see him holding his beard with one hand and flailing away at Adams with the other!"

The two old friends were still chuckling half an hour later when they arrived at the Sugar Bowl.

If you had dropped into the Sugar Bowl that night you would have thought you were entering the morgue. The gloom hung like a thick curtain over the whole place, but it was heaviest near the fountain.

Soapy was all alone and feeling low in spirits. He had tried to talk to Chip with no success. Chip wasn't talking then and he wasn't talking the next morning when his mother joined him in the living room. After several attempts to stir Chip out of his lethargy, she went directly to the heart of his problem.

"Don't worry about it, Chip," Mary Hilton said soothingly. "Everything will come out all right. Mr. Zimmerman is a nice man and a fair man. You'll see Tuesday. Just tell him the whole story."

"But, Mother, what can I say?"

"If you made a mistake, son, be a man and say so—"

"I can't say that, Mother. I don't feel that way. I'm not sorry a bit—I'd do it again!"

"If you are sure you acted rightly, Chip, then there's nothing to fear. I'm sure Mr. Zimmerman appreciates the truth and will allow for your honest convictions. Now, let's drop the matter and try to enjoy our day at home— Only, Chip dear, please promise me you won't do any more fighting. I want you to grow up to be the kind of man your father was. I'm sure he wouldn't approve of fighting even when he knew he was right."

A little later Chip left the room carrying the sports section of the *Times*. He didn't want his mother to see Muddy Waters' column, then or ever.

But Chip had forgotten about the close friendship which existed between his mother and Mrs. Browning, the kindly next-door neighbor. Coming home from church that morning, Tap's mother sympathetically tried to lift some of the worry from Mary Hilton's heart.

"Everything will come out all right, Mary," Mrs. Browning said softly. "No one pays any attention to that Waters."

"Waters?" Mary Hilton echoed. "I don't know what you mean—"

A little later, sitting in the Brownings' parlor, Mary Hilton found out what her friend meant. She read Waters' article with mounting indignation and amazement. Her gentle nature was incapable of understanding the motive behind such a story. But in spite of her reaction to the column, there was a glow of understanding in her heart as she saw another instance of the thoughtfulness of her son. Now she understood why she had been unable to find the sports page of the *Times* that morning.

After lunch, Chip studied until Soapy, Biggie, Speed, and Red showed up. They were gloomy and discouraged, still stinging from the Delford defeat. And they were bitter in their criticism of Principal Zimmerman.

Soapy was the most outspoken. "What kind of a deal

is this! What's the matter with that Zimmerman?" he demanded. "I think I'll quit school! I don't have to go to school, anyway! I know one thing I'm going to do before I quit! I'm going to see Zimmerman and tell him where to get off! That's the first game he's seen all year and he gets on us instead of Weaver and that bunch of ribbers and cheap sports. What we gonna do tomorrow? Who's gonna throw?"

No one knew the answer to Soapy's questions and the group lapsed into a deep silence which was only broken when, a little later, Petey and Paddy Jackson arrived.

Petey reported that his grandmother was much, much better. In fact, she was swell; up and around; even eating candy!

"Guess what?" he asked, after an awkward pause. "Guess who I saw last night at the pool—" Petey tried to check the last words, but it was too late.

"Last night?" his listeners chorused.

The silence which followed was heavy. Petey was thinking furiously as he hedged. "I—er—that is—I stopped by the poolroom after I found Grandma was so improved and who do you think I saw?"

Petey waited expectantly, but there was no response.

"Well, Weaver was there—" Petey shot a quick glance at Chip and continued. "Weaver was there with a black eye, and Adams, and who do you think they were talking to? Jerry Davis and Muddy Waters!"

"So what?" Soapy demanded.

"So what?" Petey echoed. "Nothing, except I heard Davis and Waters laughing about Chip falling for Weavers' come-on and all of them talking about Chip falling into the trap! Only Weaver and Adams didn't do any laughing. You know something? The whole four of them are working together to get Rock. That's the reason Waters has been riding Chip and the Rock. I've been suspicious of that tie-up ever since I saw the four of them buddying-up down there at the poolroom."

Soapy jumped to his feet. "That settles it!" he said. "I'm gonna see Zimmerman! Right now! Come on you guys!"

Petey's disclosures substantiated Chip's worst fears. This was serious . . . Maybe he ought to reconsider that election idea of his . . . Not all blue laws were silly. . . .

"Wait a minute, fellows," Chip said softly, "this is my problem, right now. At least until after I see Mr. Zimmerman on Tuesday. You've got to promise to let me work this out my way—"

"But what about the game tomorrow, Chip?" Biggie asked. "We don't have a pitcher! Remember?"

"Yeah," Speed added, "and don't forget this is Memorial Day and they celebrate it tomorrow and the stores will all be closed and there'll be a million people out there to see us play Stratford—"

"I know," Chip said patiently, "I know how important it is, but after all, I'm the one who's up to his neck in this mess—and I'd rather handle it my own way."

"Sure, Chip," Schwartz agreed, "but we want to win the game. It's your turn to pitch!"

"I want to win, too, Red," Chip said evenly, "but there's more to this than a game of baseball. Tell you what I'll do. I'll make a bargain. If you fellows will keep out of it, I'll get into politics."

Soapy got it first. "You mean you'll run for mayor?" he demanded excitedly.

Chip nodded. "That's right!" he said firmly. "I'm a candidate for mayor!"

CHAPTER 5

THE ROCK INTERVENES

THE pacing began again. Across the length of the comfortable living room to the windows facing out on the street. A short pause while black eyes under a furrowed brow peered out at the lengthening shadows of the late afternoon sun. Then back to the fireplace and another pause while worried eyes studied the clock, the pictures, and the small vase of flowers on the mantel.

"Hank," Louise Rockwell said softly, "why don't you call Mr. Zimmerman on the telephone and have a talk with him? You need to get your mind at rest. You've worried all day."

The lines of Henry Rockwell's face relaxed and his eyes softened as he checked his nervous pacing to look at his wife. Louise Rockwell was slight of build, delicate in appearance, with brownish-red hair graying at the temples, soft brown eyes, a turned-up nose and a fair complexion. It would come as a surprise to anyone to learn that she had been married to Henry Rockwell for nearly forty years.

Rockwell sighed. "I guess I'd better, Louise," he said uncertainly. "Still, I can't get the rank injustice of the whole thing out of my mind. And besides, I don't know what in the world we're going to do for a pitcher to-morrow if Zim won't let Chip play."

He moved to her side and placed a hand on her shoulder. "I'm sorry I spoiled your day, Louise," he said softly, "but we're right at the turning point of our season and every game is important. Steeltown and Salem are going great guns and we can't afford to lose more than one or two more games. I don't approve of brawling—but what Zimmerman doesn't know is that Chip got into trouble defending me! If you don't mind, I think I'll walk over to Zim's and have another talk with him."

Carl Zimmerman had been employed by the Valley Falls High School for seven years. The first six of those seven years had been pleasant in spite of the political influence which governed the school board and therefore Principal Carl Zimmerman. However, ever since Mark Condon had been elected mayor of the town the previous year, Zimmerman had been subjected to constant interference in the administration of his duties as principal of the school.

The near-riot at the game the previous day had been on his mind ever since, and he knew that come Tuesday morning, if not sooner, Mayor Condon and some of his friends on the school board would demand a full explanation. So it was understandable why Zimmerman should be a trifle reserved when Henry Rockwell visited him late that Sunday afternoon and pleaded for the reinstatement of Chip Hilton.

Zimmerman was patient but obdurate. Yes, he realized that Chip was important to the team's success and that there was no other pitcher available.

And he knew exactly the predicament in which Hank Rockwell found himself. But it was impossible for him to reinstate young Hilton without a thorough investigation of the incident.

After her husband had turned the corner and disappeared from sight, Louise Rockwell opened the Sunday issue of the *Times* to the sports page. It didn't take her long to discover the article which had disturbed Henry Rockwell earlier that morning.

DELFORD SCALPS BIG REDS, 11–0

By Muddy Waters

Hilton Suspended

Valley Falls' state champs were rudely surprised at Ohlsen Field yesterday when Delford lavishly applied a coat of whitewash to the red-faced locals. The visitors put on a three-ring circus for the near-capacity crowd of fans. They scored three runs in the opening frame and then sparkled a triple play in their first time in the field.

The locals never got over that first inning and Delford coasted to an easy victory. The expected battle of southpaws never developed. Bill Sheffer, star Delford portsider, handcuffed the Big Reds and came near to adding a no-hitter to the horse collaring, but slipped with two out in the fourth when Cohen touched him for a double. But that was as far as it went. Sheffer set Badger down on four pitches and that lone hit was all the Big Reds could get.

Hilton Attacks Fan

In the seventh inning, just after Delford took the field, William "Chip" Hilton invaded the stands to attack a fan who had been good-humoredly razzing the home forces. The suddenness of the assault shocked every person in the park and a near-riot ensued when Hilton's teammates joined him in the unwarranted attack. Combined efforts of indignant spectators and Police Officer Bob Gilbert soon broke up the melee and the players returned to the field.

Principal Zimmerman showed resolute courage when he overruled Coach Henry Rockwell in ordering hotheaded Hilton from the field, and suspended him from school. At the time this paper went to press, no information concerning possible assault charges against the erring youth had been preferred.

Louise Rockwell's eyes were snapping as she turned the page to Waters' gossip column. She always read the spiteful writer's column. Not because she was one of his fans, but because she was worried about the constant attacks Waters directed toward her husband. The very first words warned her of what was coming.

TIMES AND SPORTS

By Muddy Waters

If Coach Rockwell had the ability to develop team fight on the field instead of show-offs, there might be a slim chance for the Big Reds to successfully defend their section and state laurels . . . As it is . . .

It was just as well that the sound of footsteps on the front porch prevented Louise Rockwell from reading the rest of the vicious article. She hastily folded the paper and was placing it on the reading table just as Henry Rockwell entered the room. One look at her husband's grim face told her that the trek had been in vain; Zimmerman had not relented.

The majority of coaches spend more time working out their team and campaign plans at home than they do on the field and in their offices. And most coaches' wives join them in this extracurricular homework. Mrs. Rockwell was no exception. She knew every boy who played for her husband; knew his strength and weaknesses as well as did her husband. But she knew her husband best of all. These two had spent so much time together in such complete harmony that words were often unnecessary to express opinions or even thoughts.

Rockwell's tense face relaxed for a second and the twisted smile with which he greeted her told Louise Rockwell everything. During all the years these two had shared their lives, they had come to know and understand all the little gestures and actions which express a person's innermost emotions and feelings better than a thousand words. It was not strange then that no further reference was made to the controversy over Hilton's reinstatement.

So what should have been a day of rest from the worries of a hot baseball campaign turned out to be a frustrating, tiresome day, all the more difficult for Henry Rockwell to bear because of the inactivity. Later that evening Rockwell called Chip.

"You won't be able to play tomorrow, Chip. I talked to Mr. Zimmerman this afternoon and it looks as though there's nothing we can do about it until Tuesday. Are you planning to come to the game? . . . No? . . . Well, maybe it's just as well. I'll call you at home Tuesday morning. And, Chipper, I just want you to know that I'm with you and that I appreciate what prompted you to do what you did and that everything will come out okay—"

"Thanks, Coach." The boy's voice sounded calm and quiet over the wire. But Rockwell knew something of the turmoil that was in the youngster's heart.

Valley Falls was only a small town, but its holiday telephone business was, in proportion, just as heavy as that of a large city. So Chip's mother had no opportunity to spend the next day at home with her son. Her duties as supervisor of the local telephone exchange required her presence, holiday or no holiday.

But in spite of the pressure of work that morning in

Valley Falls, Mary Hilton found time to call John Schroeder.

"Chip is awfully upset, John, and I'm worried sick about his suspension—"

John Schroeder's familiar voice came reassuringly over the wire. "Now, Mary, there's nothing to get upset about! I saw the whole thing! I don't know exactly what started the trouble, but I know Chip and I know he had good cause for whatever action he took."

"But the paper said it was assault and—"

Schroeder's voice was calm, but there was a decided edge to the tone of his words when he interrupted. "The paper didn't say that, Mary. An unscrupulous, unreliable would-be sports writer wrote that. You are very foolish to pay any attention to anything he writes. Now you just relax and let me take care of the matter.

"By the way, the Sugar Bowl will be closed this afternoon and Petey and Chip are going to the game with Doc Jones and myself. You just forget about the whole thing. I'll call Zimmerman the first thing in the morning. Oh, yes, suppose you see that Chip stays close to the telephone tomorrow morning, so he'll be handy when Zimmerman sends for him."

That afternoon, Chip and Petey sat between John Schroeder and Doc Jones high up in the grandstand. It was the first time since he had played for Valley Falls that Chip had ever sat in the grandstand and watched the Big Reds play baseball. Two years before he had been forced to sit in the stands during part of the football season, because of a leg injury sustained in an automobile accident. Then, during the following months, he had served as manager of the basketball team. But this was the first time during four years of baseball that he had not been in uniform.

It was a strange feeling to be sitting up there with the

spectators. Chip's eyes roved over the rows of towns-people who made up the typical baseball crowd. Directly below, he saw Jerry Davis and Dick Cantwell sitting with their heads close together, talking earnestly. Something alerted Chip and he followed their glances toward the bleachers where Adams, Weaver, and their usual crowd were seated behind the home team's dugout. Instinctively, Chip felt that he was concerned in some way in the discussion and he was right.

"I don't see him," Davis was whispering to Cantwell. "Don't believe he's here."

Cantwell looked around guardedly. "Don't worry," he said in a low voice, "if he is, Buck and Peck will find him."

Meanwhile, behind the Valley Falls dugout, Buck Adams and Peck Weaver were busily scanning the field trying to locate their pet peeve number two.

"He's not in uniform, that's sure," Weaver grumbled.

Adams turned to study the rapidly filling bleachers. "Maybe he's in the crowd," he said hopefully. "Hope so. We got him on the run and we might as well keep him goin'."

A few seconds later Weaver elbowed Adams and muttered excitedly, "I've found him. He's up in the grandstand. Last row. Right next to Jones and Schroeder. See him?"

Adams nodded. "You're right! Well, looks like we'll have to pay a little visit to the grandstand."

"Not this afternoon," Weaver cautioned. "After all, Schroeder and Doc Jones are right popular guys and we gotta be careful."

"We won't do nothin'," Adams protested, "nothin' 'cept razz the grandstander a little bit. What's the harm in that?"

CHAPTER 6

GRANDSTANDER

SOAPY SMITH groaned with every warm-up pitch from
the mound and he was joined by almost every Big Reds'
rooter in the park. The fans didn't like it and Soapy
Smith didn't like it. Soapy's only baseball desire was to
catch for his idol, Chip Hilton, and the fans had come
to see the Big Reds' star keep Valley Falls in the race
for Section Two honors. But on Rockwell's orders,
Soapy had limbered up and then walked slowly across
the diamond, grumbling and worrying all the way but
determined to do his best. Then the stands began to
buzz.

"Where's Hilton? It's his turn to pitch."

"What *is* this? More of Rockwell's strategy?"

"It's not Rockwell's fault. That guy Zimmerman suspended Hilton."

"Sure, it was in the paper."

"Zimmerman's a dope!"

"That Zimmerman oughtta stick to his books!"

"What's the matter with Trullo?"

"Trullo pitched Saturday."

"So what? He's a big, strong kid."

42

"You know Rockwell—won't pitch a kid unless he's had three to four days' rest."

"Yeah, but we can't afford to lose any more games. Salem and Steeltown are tough."

"Someone ought to tell that Zimmerman where to get off."

Quite a few grandstand fans were glowering at Zimmerman now, and the remarks became more pointed. But Zimmerman seemed oblivious to everything except his conversation with Burrell Rogers, head of the physical education department and faculty supervisor of athletics.

"I don't know what to do about him, Rogers," Zimmerman said worriedly. "He's such a grand fellow but he just doesn't seem to understand that the board is determined to retire him."

Rogers nodded understandingly. "I know, Zim. I've tried to talk to him, but he's got a one-track mind. Says he's going to coach as long as he lives."

"Well," Zimmerman said, "he'd better be looking around for another job then, because Mayor Condon has the board all lined up to pension him off come the end of this term."

"What about Ohlsen and Jim Stanton and George Thomas? Condon has to have a majority, doesn't he?"

"Sure, but he controls the deciding vote, ex officio."

"That's right! I hadn't thought of that! Sure hate to see Hank go."

A park-filling roar brought their attention back to the game. Soapy was already in trouble. The Stratford lead-off hitter had punched a wobbly Texas leaguer right over third and had taken second when Lefty Peters couldn't field the ball in time for a play. That upset Soapy and he walked the next two batters. Like the Big Reds' Biggie Cohen, Stratford's first sacker was a lefty and batted in the cleanup spot. He was loose up there and Soapy made the mistake of trying to throw one past him. The tall, lanky boy met the fast ball right on the nose, pulling it over Biggie Cohen's head in a low liner which hit fifty feet beyond the sack and rolled all the way to the right-field fence just inside the foul line.

Nick Trullo was after the ball with the crack of the bat, but misjudged the rebound from the fence and three runs scored, the hitter holding up at third. Before the side was retired the cleanup hitter scored also, and when the Big Reds came in for their licks they were behind 4 to 0. And when the stretch inning finally arrived, Stratford was leading, 7 to 0. The visitors' chucker had blanked everyone except Biggie Cohen; he had never been in trouble.

Chip's thoughts were bitter as he squirmed in his seat high up in the grandstand. The loss of this game would practically eliminate the Big Reds from the race for the defense of its championship. Right now Salem was leading Section Two, with Steeltown right on their heels. It was too bad they had lost to Steeltown a little earlier in the season at Steeltown. It had been a great game and Trullo had pitched well, but the loss was on the books. If Stratford won this game—and it now seemed a cinch that they would—it would mean three defeats and only six victories. And there were still six tough games to come. It didn't look good.

Chip could hear Adams and Weaver riding Rockwell relentlessly and a surge of anger flooded his thoughts. If it hadn't been for those two roughnecks, these last two home games might have been won.

Adams and Weaver again had been unsuccessful in their attempts to get a rise out of Rockwell and now decided to pay Chip Hilton a visit in the grandstand. They brazenly climbed over the railing which separated the first-base bleachers from the grandstand and shoved their way into the last row of seats. From their new location they began to bait Chip, not directly, but by obvious reference.

"Right where he belongs—in the grandstand!"

"Yeah, once a grandstander, always a grandstander!"

"Notice he always has himself well surrounded."

"Yeah, quite a fighter, when he has a gang with him."

Chip clenched his fists and tried to concentrate upon the play on the field. But it required all his self-control and only the memory of the promise he had made his mother enabled him to disregard the thinly veiled insults. Several times Petey Jackson gripped Chip's arm in sympathetic understanding.

Doc Jones and John Schroeder were angry, too, but they retained their composure. Long years of experience had taught them that such matters always balanced themselves out, one way or another.

Stu Gardner was deeply interested in this grandstand byplay. He recognized Adams and Weaver for what they were, knew the whole background of their feud with Rockwell, and his sympathies were all with the veteran coach and Chip Hilton. Gardner no longer was concerned about Chip Hilton's emotional balance. He marveled at the kid's self-control and he wondered at the stories he had heard about the feud between the South Side roughnecks and Chip Hilton.

A quick, fleeting appraisal of hard-faced Peck Weaver and his counterpart, Buck Adams, was usually enough for most casual observers. But it took some time to evaluate the physical make-up of the men. And Gardner critically studied Weaver, noting the mean eyes, breadth of shoulders, long arms, wide, meaty hands, and thick body. Stu Gardner shifted his eyes from Weaver to the slender youngster sitting there in the grandstand and he shook his head in disbelief. It just didn't add up in Gardner's book. How did that kid, six-two and probably weighing no more than one-eighty, ever best Weaver in a stand-up fight? Not once, but twice, according to the stories he had heard.

Gardner knew the kid was fast and in good shape, but those assets were nothing compared to Weaver's forty-pound weight advantage and his experience in rough-and-tumble brawling. Anyway, the kid sure had nerve! Going over on the South Side hill all alone and challenging Peck Weaver to a fair fight! Most young-sters would have taken one look at the roughneck, piv-oted, and headed for home—fast!

When the dreary game finally ended, Chip cast a mournful eye at the 10–1 trouncing recorded on the scoreboard and silently trailed his three friends out of the grandstand. And he was still quiet when he clam-bered in beside Petey in the back seat of John Schroe-der's car. He was glad Adams and Weaver hadn't tricked him into another mistake; glad he had been able to keep his head. The whole plot was clear to him now, and he wasn't going to be stupid enough to fall for their bait again. He himself wasn't important at all. They were after Rockwell. Well, they had played him for a fool and he had fallen for it the first time—but that would be the last. And he had a plan that might help to even the score. If he could win the election . . . If he could stay in school. . . .

The Sugar Bowl closed early on holiday evenings and Chip thankfully headed straight for home that night to do some studying. Strangely enough, none of the Hil-ton A. C. members were around to walk along with him. Chip gave it little thought; he wanted to get home, hit the books, and ready himself for the meeting with Principal Zimmerman the next day.

Chip would have been astonished if he had been able to see the gathering in the kitchen at Soapy Smith's house that night. Petey Jackson was holding forth at the kitchen table and listening intently were Biggie Cohen, Red Schwartz, Taps Browning, Speed Morris, and Soapy.

"Soapy and I have our part all set," Petey said proudly. "See, here's the slips. All you guys gotta do is get 'em in the hands of the right people. Soapy, you got the list?"

"Now, look. I'll call out the names and you let me know which ones you'll take. Write 'em down! All set?"

Half an hour later Petey sighed. "Well, that's that," he said grimly. "How much is one hundred and eighty times twenty-five cents? How much? *Forty-five bucks!*"

"Yep, forty-five smackers," Soapy echoed. "But it'll only cost you twenty-two fifty, personally. We're in this deal fifty-fifty, you know. That's my whole month's salary!"

"You mean if Chip wins the election it'll cost you twenty-two fifty," Biggie reminded them. "If Chip isn't elected, it won't cost you anything."

"He'll win," Soapy said stoutly, "and we'll pay! Don't worry about that! Remember, though, it's in trade."

"Yeah, and they gotta collect the night of the election," Petey warned.

Speed laughed. "It'll be a madhouse," he said gleefully. "A regular madhouse!"

Schwartz was nearly hysterical. "Oh, boy," he chortled, "wait'll Schroeder sees that mob. Can you imagine a hundred and eighty seniors trying to get into the Sugar Bowl all at once. Oh, boy!"

While Chip's friends were working on the Independent party platform and perfecting their plans to sway the voting desires of one hundred and eighty Valley

Falls High School seniors, Jerry Davis was proceeding with his campaign against Henry Rockwell. And the result of Davis' Memorial Day effort was reflected in the telephone call Principal Zimmerman received from Mayor Condon at precisely nine o'clock Tuesday morning.

Zimmerman's voice was tinny and the hand holding the telephone receiver shook. "Yes, sir, I realize it's a disciplinary matter, but two weeks seems a little—

"But, Mayor, that would take him right up to the last game of the season—

"I have it right here. Let's see— Well, the season ends with the Steeltown game on the nineteenth. How about a one-week suspension? That would make him eligible for the Dulane game next Saturday."

Zimmerman's lips were pressed tightly together as the harsh, precise words echoed loudly through the receiver. When Condon finished, the worried frown lines on his brow had relaxed slightly and some relief was apparent in the tone of his voice as he completed the conversation. "Yes, sir. That's right, sir. One week, ending Friday, June 4th. Good-bye, your honor."

Ten minutes later Henry Rockwell appeared in Zimmerman's office. Rockwell was fuming and angry. He wanted Chip Hilton reinstated immediately.

"Those fellows started that fight, Zim. They used the kid to get at me. You *must* realize that!"

"That may be, Hank," Zimmerman said quietly, "but don't forget there's a matter of discipline involved. Hilton went up into the stands and every student at the game saw him. I can't bring him back and excuse him just like that—I've *got* to penalize him. We'll have to suspend him for at least a week. That's all there is to it."

Later, a disgruntled Rockwell called Chip. "Chip," he said, "I'm sorry. You've been suspended from baseball until Saturday, June 5th. I know just how you feel; I know that this is unfair, but just the same, I can't do anything about it. We'll have to grin and bear it and hope for the best. By the way, Chipper, you hustle over to Zimmerman's office and get back in school."

"Isn't there some way I can get back for Wednesday's game, Coach?"

"No. We'll have to do the best we can, Chip. You just stick it out and sit up there in the stands and give us all the moral support you can."

So Wednesday afternoon, Chip was again in the grandstand with John Schroeder and Doc Jones. And once again Buck Adams and Peck Weaver got on Rockwell; resumed their baiting and jeering. But Rockwell ignored them completely. This was an important game and he and the Big Reds went all out in their effort to win.

Nick Trullo pitched well enough, but the hitters couldn't bunch their hits and when the last Big Red went down swinging in the bottom of the ninth, Valley Falls had lost its third game in a row and fourth of the season.

Muddy Waters took full advantage of the opportunity the next day and what he said wasn't nice. Soapy and Petey were leaning against the soda fountain, pouring over the *Times*.

"Look at this!" Petey growled, jabbing a long, skinny forefinger into the page. "How *about* this guy!"

TIMES AND SPORTS

By Muddy Waters

Good-bye state and section championships . . . Delford probably took care of that yesterday afternoon at Ohlsen Field. . . . The 5–2 score indicates how far and how fast the Big Reds have slipped . . . Delford has a season over-all record of *three* wins and eight losses . . . Gives you a pretty good idea of the Big Reds' vulnerability.

Chip Hilton's bleacher escapade now begins to assume serious proportions for the Big Reds. . . . Hilton's presence in the line-up in the last three games *might* have kept Valley Falls in the race . . . Then again it might not have made any difference.

Some athletes can handle success . . . Some can't . . . Some athletes confine their fighting spirit to the play of the game . . . Some don't . . . one swelled head can ruin a team.

Many fans are wondering what kind of alibi Coach Henry Rockwell will come up with this time.

Remember last year's state gridiron championship? . . . What happened this year? . . . Nine regulars returned.

Remember last year's state hoop championship? . . . What happened this year? . . . The varsity five returned intact.

Remember last year's state diamond championship? . . . What's happening this year? . . . All but one regular is in uniform. . . . By the way . . . The Big Reds have scored just three runs in their last three games . . . Their opponents have tallied twenty-six.

Chip Hilton's suspension ends Friday . . . Rockwell will undoubtedly start the *bleacher champion* against Dulane . . . Wouldn't it be smart to equip Hilton with a pair of ear muffs? . . . Or should Rockwell address the Dulane fans just before the game and ask them to refrain from rooting because it upsets his temperamental star?

Soapy crumpled the paper in his hands and began to tear it to pieces. "Why, that—that—that—"

Whatever Soapy meant to say was never finished. This was one of the few times in his career Soapy was at a loss for words. But words weren't important right then. Petey Jackson knew exactly what his fountain assistant meant. And Petey was completely in sympathy with Soapy's final gesture when he scooped up the bits of torn paper and threw them deliberately across the fountain and out on the floor.

Chip, in the back of the store, had heard the explosion from the vicinity of the soda fountain and had watched Soapy's destructive fury in amusement. But the shower of paper on the floor which he was supposed to keep immaculate roused him into action. He hurried forward.

"Hey, what goes?" he demanded. "What's the idea?"

Soapy glared at Chip for a second and then the words came. "Jerk! Bum! No good stupe! Crackpot! Half-wit! Half-baked imbecile! Jerk!"

Soapy spluttered, futile fury written on his scarlet face, bringing out every freckle as if it were confetti.

Petey answered Chip's questioning glance. "Muddy Waters," he said disgustedly. "He's riding you and Rock again."

Chip nodded. "Yes, I know—well, I guess I had it coming." He turned toward Soapy and gestured toward the littered floor. "Come on, clean that up!"

Soapy cleaned it up, muttering and growling, and all that evening he bewildered his customers by referring continually in half-smothered tones to "the bum, the crackpot, the stupe, the jerk."

CHAPTER 7

BIG-LEAGUE SCOUT

STU GARDNER had been in Valley Falls only a short time, but he had learned a great deal about Coach Henry Rockwell. From idle conversations, by direct discussion and through observation, Gardner knew Rockwell to be a solid citizen, a fine family man, a coach who loved his work, and a sincerely friendly person. Still, he felt slightly ill at ease as he waited outside Rockwell's office.

A few minutes later, however, all his awkwardness was dispelled by Rockwell's warm greeting.

"Glad to know you, Gardner," Rockwell said in a friendly voice. A welcoming smile played around his lips for a brief moment while his keen, black eyes studied the card Gardner had handed him. "With the Drakes, eh? Good outfit! Sit down."

"Guess you know Del Bennett—" Gardner began.

"Sure do! Known him for years. Fine fellow! Friend of yours?"

"Sure is, coach, and that's why I got him to write this letter. Mind reading it?"

Rockwell took the letter and read it carefully.

STATE UNIVERSITY

Department of Athletics

May 28

DEAR ROCK:

This note will introduce Stu Gardner. Stu is an old friend and a former teammate of mine when I was playing ball and knew all the answers. I've found out since then that even Abner Doubleday didn't know them all. Anyway, I learned long ago that Stu Gardner was a number one right fellow and that's the reason for this letter.

Stu is interested in a couple of your kids (who isn't?) and wanted a letter of introduction. Give him all the breaks you can, but don't let him sign up that Hilton kid if there's any chance of the youngster coming up here to school. Anyway, Stu won't pull any fast ones and I think it's swell you two fellows can get acquainted. Hope to see you up here for the championships.

> *Best regards,*
> DEL BENNETT
> *Coach of Baseball*

Rockwell folded the letter slowly and laid it on his desk. "Del's a great guy," he said softly, a grin on his face, "but I didn't need the letter. I had you spotted a couple of weeks ago. Was expecting some of you fellows to show up as soon as Hilton and Cohen and a couple of the other kids got ready to graduate. Well, what's on your mind?"

Gardner wasted no words. "You named them," he said simply, "Hilton and Cohen!"

Rockwell sighed. "Yes, they've got it, Gardner. They're big league all right, but they're both planning to go to college and I'm pulling hard for them to do just that—" He spread his hands flat on the desk and leaned forward, face suddenly sober, black eyes staring hard into Gardner's. "You go for that, too, don't you, Gardner?"

Gardner tilted his head sideways and nodded reluctantly. "Well, yes, coach, I go for the college deal if a kid is a good student and wants the education." He breathed deeply, trying to hide the disappointment in his voice before continuing. "But sometimes a kid is better off taking advantage of his opportunities when they come. Especially if money is important to the family, as it appears to be in the case of these kids."

"You have something there, Gardner, but I've made it my business to find out that the parents of those boys, and the boys themselves, are looking forward to a college education. They're both good students, they're ambitious, and don't forget they'll be little more than kids when they finish college. They'll have lots of time left for professional baseball."

Rockwell studied Gardner closely. What he saw in the veteran scout's face must have pleased him, for the hard, set expression on his own face softened.

"Look here, Stu," he said kindly, "I know this is a big disappointment to you and I know exactly how you must feel. And just because I like you and like the way you do business, I'm going to get you acquainted with those two kids right away. Naturally, I expect you to refrain from trying to get them to sign a contract or even to broach your desire to sign them up until after graduation. Okay? Then, if anything ever goes wrong with their college plans, you'll at least have a speaking acquaintance with them and probably have the inside track. And as I said before, college years fly by pretty fast and they'll still be kids anyway when they get through. You'll have the contact and their confidence. Okay?"

On Friday the *Yellow Jacket* carried an announcement of the formation of the Independent party with Chip Hilton in the chief political role. The minute the paper was placed on sale, Soapy and his committeemen went to work. Soapy and the unexpected political move created surprise and indignation in the ranks of the Home Rule party and Citizens party and they almost forgot their own campaigns in the excitement. Chip's teammates were enthusiastic and once again Henry Rockwell's baseball team seemed destined for a call-down because of its political fervor. But Rockwell's mind was on Saturday's game with Dulane and he didn't notice the byplay.

The Big Reds were surprised Saturday morning, June 5th, to see a sun-bronzed stranger join Rockwell in the front seat of the bus when it pulled out for Dulane. There was some speculation concerning his identity, but the reinstatement of Chip and the lift his return had given the team were too important to arouse very much curiosity in the appearance of a stranger. The Big Reds were intact again and Soapy expressed their feelings when he said, "Salem and Steeltown may not know it, but their honeymoon is over!"

That afternoon Stu Gardner sat in the Valley Falls dugout throughout the game. He didn't talk to Rockwell nor to the players, just sat there as quietly and as unobtrusively as possible.

Coming home that night the big bus rolled steadily along and the singing and the chatter kept pace with the speeding wheels. The Big Reds were on the prowl again and everyone was in step. Chip was tired but happy. He had never felt better than that afternoon out on the hill. He had all his stuff and for the first time there had been no razzing by Weaver and Adams from the stands. For a brief moment this thought worried him, but he quickly dismissed it. Why spoil a wonderful day with thoughts of fellows of that stripe? Hadn't he pitched a no-hitter that afternoon?

At exactly nine thirty the bus stopped in front of the Sugar Bowl to disgorge the happy ballplayers who were immediately mobbed by a loyal crowd of rooters.

Rockwell checked Chip and Biggie as they were leaving the bus and asked them to drop over to his house the next day to meet a friend. So they were there the following afternoon at three o'clock, not a little surprised to find the stranger who had made the trip with the team to Dulane sitting on the porch with the Rock and Mrs. Rockwell.

After the introductions, Mrs. Rockwell excused herself and Henry Rockwell took charge of the conversation.

"Boys, Mr. Gardner here is a scout for the Drakes and he's been watching you fellows for a couple of weeks hoping he could sign you to contracts as soon as you were graduated."

Gardner smiled ruefully. "That's right, fellows, I had hopes of signing you for our chain, but the coach kinda put the damper on that— Said you were planning to go to college." He paused expectantly, but the two boys were nonplused. They looked uncertainly at one another and it was Rockwell who broke the awkward silence.

"That's right, isn't it, Chip?"

Both boys nodded and then Rockwell continued. "I thought it would be a good chance for you to learn something about big-league opportunities. Contracts and bonuses and all that. Stu, suppose you tell us about the procedure the big leagues follow with respect to signing high school boys to contracts."

Gardner took over then, and for the next hour explained big-league legislation with respect to signing high school players, the bonus, and other rules. He explained that unscrupulous scouts often signed boys secretly and that the commissioner of baseball had the power to revoke such contracts. When he had finished, Gardner asked the boys if they had any questions.

"I'm going to have a tough time getting through college," Biggie said hesitatingly, "and I've been wondering if big-league teams ever sign up fellows who want to go on to college."

"Yes, that's been done. There's no rule against that. Of course such a player would be ineligible for college baseball," Gardner explained. "You see, as soon as a boy signs a big-league contract, he becomes a professional. Quite a few players have been signed after they got through high school and have been paid a monthly salary while they were in college. But they didn't play college baseball. And, I suppose, a few have been signed up secretly and still played college ball. But it wasn't honest and it wasn't ethical."

Shortly afterward, Chip and Biggie thanked Rockwell and Gardner and headed for the Sugar Bowl. They had learned a lot about big-league organization and administration that afternoon and each was excited by thoughts that someday he might have the opportunity to sign a contract and get a bonus and do all the things he had dreamed about. But first, there was college and an education.

Chip was thinking about something Rock had said and he could still hear Rockwell's earnest voice: "An education is an asset which a fellow can never dissipate; *no one can take it away from him! Money and friends may vanish but an education sticks forever!*"

CHAPTER 8

STINGAROO! STINGARII! STINGAREE!

EARLY Monday morning Rockwell received a call from Principal Zimmerman's office. "Now what?" Rockwell muttered as he made his way along the broad hall to the school's main office. A call so early in the morning was unusual and Rockwell had a hunch it meant more trouble. Zimmerman's first words substantiated the presentiment.

"I've got some bad news for you, Hank."

Rockwell's brow furrowed deeply as he looked at Zimmerman. "You don't mean Hilton again?"

"Er—well, not entirely, Hank," Zimmerman said slowly. "Something more important. I hate to tell you this, Hank, but I think you ought to know that Jerry Davis and Waters and the rest of the crowd who have been after your scalp are—well—making progress."

Rockwell shook his head impatiently. "Don't let that

58

worry you, Zim. They can't hurt me. The Board of Education has the last say on that score and I've known J. P. Ohlsen and Jim Stanton and George Thomas for thirty years. They're my best friends!"

"But how about old man Davis and Frank Greer and Fred Cantwell?"

"Well, they're not my friends, Zim, but they have no reason to dislike me—none that I know of, at any rate."

Zimmerman shrugged. "Maybe not, Hank, but don't forget that Davis is Jerry's father—and that Greer and Cantwell side with him in everything."

"Sure, but they only make up half the board, and it takes a majority to pass on a retirement decision."

"Yes, Hank, but I happen to know that a lot of pressure is being put on Mayor Condon and he's ex officio chairman of the board."

"I'll never quit," Rockwell said thinly.

"You'll have to quit sometime, Hank, and you've had a great career. Your pension will amount to nearly as much as your salary. What have you got to lose?"

"Money isn't everything," Rockwell said grimly. "No, Zim, I just happen to like my job."

"But you're past retirement age, Hank, and besides, you've been here thirty-eight years."

"Thirty-seven," Rockwell growled.

"Well, thirty-seven then, Rock, but you know that the law states that a teacher who reaches the age of sixty-three *must* be retired. Furthermore, it states that a teacher who has served thirty-five years in the public school system must *also* be retired. You qualify on both counts."

"Qualify! Huh! What about a man's ability to do a good job? You mean to tell me that any other man, young or old, knows more about my job or will do a better job than I can do with all the years of experience

I've had? Do you think some youngster will know more about kids than I know?"

"No, Rock, I don't believe that at all. But I don't have the say on this matter and I just wanted to let you know what you're up against."

Rockwell grunted. "They're up against something, too. They won't force me out if I can help it." He shrugged his shoulders impatiently. "What would I do? I'd go crazy!"

There was a long silence as each was busy with his own thoughts. Rockwell finally broke the silence.

"You said something about Chip—"

"Oh, yes, but it's not very important."

"Anything which concerns Chip Hilton's important, Zim, you know that! He's the difference! The difference between a good baseball team and an ordinary one."

"It's not about baseball, Hank. It's about the kid's political campaign. He's the Independent party's candidate for mayor, and, well, in view of his recent difficulties, I'm afraid I can't permit it."

"But, Zim, that's not fair! What's the baseball incident got to do with the senior political campaign. The kid's been penalized enough! He was out of baseball for three games! And he's a student in good standing!"

"It *is* fair, Hank. The boy was reinstated in baseball and that's enough." Zimmerman's voice was firm and a bit testy as he continued. "The administration of student activities is solely in my hands, Hank, and that's my decision."

Rockwell could not shake Zimmerman's determined stand and he left the office thoroughly disgusted with Zimmerman and his extravagant ideas concerning discipline. The Rock was thinking that there were a number of unusual situations and changes developing at Valley Falls High School which he didn't like and which he could not understand. Zim acted almost as though he were afraid for his job, or something. . . .

Zimmerman could have cleared up all of the veteran mentor's uncertainty if he had felt it wise to disclose the nature of another telephone call he had received from the mayor of Valley Falls at his home that very morning. Condon had insisted that the newly formed Independent party in the high school be disbanded at once.

"I won't have this splendid student activity turned into a farce," the mayor had fumed. "The party must be outlawed immediately, and the Hilton boy withdrawn from the campaign!"

Zimmerman could only agree to comply with the order, but rebellion against this unnecessary interference was building up in his heart and in his mind with each passing day. The position he held was becoming unendurable and Zimmerman resolved to try to make some contacts which might result in an opportunity where duties apropos to the government of the city would be more important to politicians than the persecution of a boy who had incurred some political friend's displeasure.

Rockwell's bitter mood carried over into practice that afternoon. It was reflected in the crisp tones of his voice and in his impatient orders.

Chip didn't know what was wrong with Rockwell, but he knew what had dampened his own spirits. Zimmerman had tried to soften the blow, but the decision had been hard to take and Chip had walked out of the principal's office and back to his home room badly hurt. He had said nothing then to his friends and he said nothing that afternoon when Zimmerman called a special assembly and announced that the Independent party was being withdrawn from the campaign.

But Soapy and Biggie and Speed and Red didn't take it without comment. They were up in arms and they had plenty of support. The suddenness of the blow had floored Soapy and his only recourse was a strong verbal condemnation of Zimmerman.

"Why, that jerk," he exploded, "that jerk!" And that was the extent of Soapy's reaction to Zimmerman's announcement at the time. But his agile mind was busy through practice that afternoon.

The futility of the whole thing affected the Big Reds' practice session that afternoon, too, and Rockwell was smart enough to realize that the workout was wasted effort. After a brief hitting practice and an even shorter fielding drill, he sent them twice around the field and then to the showers.

That night the Sugar Bowl was quiet and deserted. None of the ballplayers were around and those who know them best would have been surprised, particularly Chip Hilton, if they could have seen the "council of war" at Soapy Smith's house. With the exception of Chip, every member of the Hilton A. C. was on hand, as well as every member of the ball club. As usual, it was Soapy who was doing most of the talking.

"Look," he said, "I got an idea!"

"Treat it gently," Biggie growled. "It's in a strange place!"

Soapy sent a withering look in Biggie's direction. "No cracks," he commanded, "this is serious! Dead serious! Look, we're gonna beat that jerk Zimmerman at his own game! We're gonna elect Chip, anyway—"

"But Zimmerman threw the party out," someone said.

"So what! Now look, we gotta hurry! We've got to call up every kid in town. Zimmerman can't stop us from voting the way we want to! That's why they have the little booths; so a guy can vote the way he wants!"

"Our constitution and our whole government's been built on voting the way we feel." Soapy beamed self-consciously, then continued proudly, "Why, my last theme for old Sourpuss Mitchell was about democratic voting procedure and he told me it was the best paper he got all term—grade A!"

Everyone groaned, but Soapy merely lifted his eyebrows in disdain. "Well," he demanded, "don't you believe it?"

Schwartz chuckled. "Well, maybe," he said, "but what about Republican voting procedure?" he asked, grinning broadly.

"They're democratic, too," Soapy said decisively. "Now, listen—"

While Chip's friends listened, Soapy unfolded his plan to outwit Zimmerman and assure the election of Chip Hilton. And in other homes, boys and girls were talking about the enforced withdrawal of Chip Hilton from the senior campaign. A few of the interested persons were gloating; exultant because of the unexpected ouster of a dangerous candidate. But there were many who didn't like it and these were wondering if there weren't something they could do about it.

Among those who gloated because of the elimination of Chip Hilton from the election were Jerry Davis, Muddy Waters, several of their cronies—and particularly Buck Adams and Peck Weaver.

"I wish we could fix that kid's wagon once and for all!" Weaver said venomously.

"Maybe we can," Adams said thoughtfully. "I been thinkin' maybe we could frame him into another fight and then get Davis to put some pressure on the mayor and get Hilton thrown out of school."

"You think Condon could make Zimmerman do that?"

Adams laughed contemptuously. "You kiddin'?" he

asked. "Look, Condon's got that guy in the palm of his hand. Sure he'd do it!"

"Well, then, what are we waitin' for?"

"Nothin' much, except we don't want to make any mistakes. We gotta be careful. The kid's popular and we don't want to have any run-ins with the law right now."

"I got it!" Weaver said suddenly. "Look, we'll tell Gilbert—he's the only cop they ever send to the games—we'll tell him Hilton has been threatenin' us, see? Tell him the kid said he was gonna get us with his gang. Then we'll get Hilton steamed up at one of the games. Let's see, the Steeltown game's scheduled here for the sixteenth. That's it! We'll set it up for the sixteenth! Then we'll frame Hilton and when he jumps us we'll have Gilbert to back us up. Get it?"

Adams slapped Weaver on the back. "Hey," he said with exaggerated surprise in his voice, "you're gettin' smart! That's just the ticket! We'll tell Gilbert we don't want no trouble with Hilton and ask him to watch out when we go to the games."

"Yeah, but what if he hears us razzin' Hilton?"

"So what? Everyone razzes ballplayers. What we want to do is get Hilton mad and make him climb up in the stands again. See what I mean? Then Davis can have Condon step in and make Zimmerman throw Hilton outta school—and Rockwell will be up against it for pitchers and the town'll get on him—and we'll be rid of both of those guys for good."

Tuesday's classes at Valley Falls High School might just as well have been dismissed. Principal Zimmerman and his staff of teachers expected the day before the senior election to be eventful; they had gone through the experience before and were prepared for the worst. But they had never experienced anything like this election eve. In every class and home room one topic and one topic only was of interest to the students: the election. After vain attempts to stick to their course schedules, most of the instructors threw up their hands and turned their class periods over to the politicians.

Coach Henry Rockwell believed that a noisy dressing room filled with happy baseball chatter was an indication of good team spirit and the trade-mark of a championship team. So, that afternoon as he dressed in his office there was a satisfied smile on his face as he listened to the excited voices and loud laughter in the Big Reds' dressing room below. But the smile faded a few minutes later when he descended the steps to the locker room and listened to the conversation.

"Can't miss! Bet they don't get ten votes!"

"Gotta get ten; there's twelve of 'em running."

"Okay, then twelve!"

"Hey, Soapy! What you gonna do for money next month?"

The clackety-clack, clack-clack of Rockwell's spikes on the iron staircase usually subdued the clamor, but not this afternoon. He wasn't even noticed. Striding past old Pop without a side glance, and without his usual, "Hello, Pop," Rockwell slammed out the door. The veteran trainer looked after him fearfully. "Someone's gonna catch it," he muttered. "Gonna catch it good! Wonder what's wrong with *him?*"

Chip was dressing quietly in front of his locker. He had tried all day to be cheerful, conceal the hurt in his heart. And he had tried to laugh with the others and get into the swing of the election excitement, but it was no go. So he had given up; had tried to concentrate his thoughts on the game tomorrow with Parkton. However, the evident relish with which Biggie, Soapy, Speed, and Red entered into the elections had him puzzled. And although he knew each of his friends almost as well as he knew himself, he couldn't figure out why they were so excited.

Out on the field a little later Rockwell tried to dope it out, too. He knew his team was up to something, but it wasn't baseball. For a second his temper flared; nearly burst into a flame of criticism, burning words of condemnation. But second thought brought him back to the realization that these boys were concerned right then with something which was more important than practice, Henry Rockwell, and the game with Parkton. "It's the election," he whispered to himself, "sure as shooting! They're up to something and it concerns Chip!"

Rockwell noticed that Chip took no part in the discussions, and that gave him an inkling to the mystery. "Of course," he whispered again, "that's it! They're going to pull a fast one in the election. They're going to outmaneuver Zimmerman. I knew they wouldn't let Chip down. Well, whatever it is, I hope it's good and that it works."

That night Chip was further bewildered by the political enthusiasm of the Hilton A. C. and by the activity which centered around the Sugar Bowl. Along the street, cars filled with students passed in front of the store all evening with the riders shouting, "Stingaroo! Stingarii! Stingaree!"

Speed's jalopy was all painted with big question marks and it was parked right out in front. And all evening Big Red seniors came into the Sugar Bowl and talked mysteriously with Soapy Smith and Petey Jackson.

Chip kept pretty much to the storeroom that evening, but like John Schroeder, he was mystified by the constant parade. Both would have been completely bewildered if they could have heard the conversations.

"What kind of a slip you want? A twenty-five center, two dimers, and a nickel, or five nickels? We're at your service!"

"You mean we got a choice?"

"Yep! You can have a slip for a quarter in trade and that means five small cokes all at once, or a milk shake and a coke, or a hamburger, or a fudge sundae, or an orangeade and two cokes, or a float— Heck, there's the soda list. Remember now: Stingaroo, stingarii, stingaree!"

Mary Hilton and her telephone operators never had a busier afternoon. All over town telephones were ringing, and in practically every instance, it was concerned with a high school senior. Chip's mother was a very tired woman when she finally started home. But it didn't end there. The night operators called her a little later to say that they would have to have more help; they just couldn't keep up with the local calls.

Wednesday morning was unusually quiet for an election day. Except for "stingaroo, stingarii, stingaree," which appeared on every blackboard and which was whispered when most seniors passed, the lack of election spirit was absolutely uncanny. That afternoon, when classes were suspended for the voting, Principal Zimmerman followed the seniors along the main hall to Ohlsen Gymnasium. Zimmerman knew boys and girls, especially the Valley Falls High School seniors. But as he stood at the door of Ohlsen gym viewing the procession of voters filing in and out of the voting booths which stood in the center of the basketball court, he sensed that *something* was wrong; it was too quiet. And what in the deuce was this "stingaroo, stingarii, stingaree" stuff?

Zimmerman was right about something being wrong and he might have been able to stop that *something* if he could have seen the headline the editors of the *Yellow Jacket* were planning for the front page of the special election issue which was to come out that afternoon.

The Big Reds' dressing room was seething as the boys dressed for the game against Parkton. Runners kept dashing in with mysterious messages then and all during the Parkton game. Chip sensed something was up, but he was too intent upon his pitching to care. Right now he wanted to get out on the mound and keep Valley Falls in the running for Section Two honors. Still, he couldn't help feeling a bit of resentment that his teammates should consider *anything* more important than the game.

Rockwell had told both of his pitchers to warm up, but when the game began it was Chip who toed the rubber. The choice was right and Chip was right. He had the Parkton hitters handcuffed. Inning after inning passed and the visiting batters were so helpless that the Parkton cleanup hitter just about expressed their futility when he said, "He owns us!"

At the top of the ninth, when Chip flashed the first strike across the plate, the score was Valley Falls 7, Parkton 1. And five minutes later there had been no change when Soapy slipped the game ball in his hip pocket and dashed up the alley toward a startled Chip Hilton. But Soapy wasn't the only one dashing toward Valley Falls' star chucker. Nor was he the only one shouting, "*Hiya, Mayor!*"

CHAPTER 9

POLITICS AND EDUCATION

THE crowd extended clear down to the corner and inside the Sugar Bowl the eager seniors were shoulder to shoulder. And inside or outside it was a noisy crowd. Behind the fountain, Soapy, Petey, Red, Speed, and Chip were swamped with orders and arguments.

"Five cokes! That's right! Put 'em all in one big glass!"

"—and strawberries and whipped cream, too!"

"I didn't say marshmallows! I said whipped cream!"

"Hey, where's the banana split?"

"At last! Go out to the farm for that milk?"

"I hear you! Three frosteds, two chocolate sodas, four nut sundaes—All right, five then, and two hamburgers, right? And with onions!"

"How come you didn't get help? You knew Chip was gonna win, didn't ya?"

"You *did* say marshmallow! Anyway, we're out of whipped cream."

"Look, I gotta have the slip! Soapy, you get his slip? No? Well then, brother, you're outta luck! Bet you didn't even vote!"

Soapy and Petey's victory slips came in; every one of

them, that night! Biggie and Speed, Paddy and Soapy, Petey and Chip, and everybody else helped out with the serving. John Schroeder and Doc Jones were amazed as they pushed their way through the crowd.

"What's this all about?" Schroeder demanded. "What in the world has happened? What are all these slips of paper for—?"

Jones shook his head vigorously. "Beats me," he said, "I don't get it."

Soapy and Petey both tried to explain at once. "Er— well, Mr. Schroeder—" Soapy began, "you see—"

"Chip was elected mayor!" Petey interrupted triumphantly. "And we're paying off!"

"Yeah—I mean yes, sir, and these slips of paper— well, they represent the pay-off—"

"And you can take it out of our wages."

John Schroeder was an understanding man but right now it suited his purpose to pretend that he didn't comprehend. "I don't get this at all," he stated sternly, turning to look meaningly at Doc Jones. "Do you get it, Doc?"

Doc Jones shook his head again. "I *still* don't get it!"

Schroeder glanced around the milling crowd of high school seniors. "Looks like the senior prom! All right, you two, hustle back and wait on them. But soon as they leave, you come back to my office! Skip the register, and put the slips on the stick file."

Schroeder and Jones managed to get through the mob and into the storeroom. There they began to laugh, and they were still laughing when Soapy and Petey appeared an hour later.

"Here you are, Mr. Schroeder," Soapy said worriedly. "Here's the special election issue of the *Yellow Jacket*. Explains everything."

"Everything but the slips of paper we been getting

out front," Petey added. "Read the paper, Mr. Schroeder, first—"

Schroeder took the paper and Doc Jones inched his chair closer. Varied emotions were expressed on their faces as they read.

THE YELLOW JACKET
VALLEY FALLS HIGH SCHOOL
June 9

Special Edition   *Vol. 31. No. 34*

CHIP HILTON ELECTED MAYOR
HILTON A. C. POLITICAL COUP SUCCESSFUL
Write-in Tactics Win

The Home Rule and Citizens parties were completely submerged this afternoon when the popular vote of the senior class shifted overwhelmingly to elect William "Chip" Hilton, the Big Reds' pitching star, to the office of mayor for the administration of the town's business on Friday, June 18. Chip was a former candidate on the Independent ticket which Principal Zimmerman ruled ineligible last Monday. The write-in vote sets a precedent and moves Hilton and his write-in associates into absolute control of the school's senior politics.

Hilton, himself, was completely in the dark with respect to the coup and was as much puzzled by the slogan adopted, "Stingaroo, Stingarii, Stingaree," as were the powers behind the Home Rule and Citizens parties.

A celebration is scheduled for tonight at the successful candidate's headquarters, the Sugar Bowl. This celebration will undoubtedly eclipse anything of its kind ever held in the history of Valley Falls High School politics. If you know what we mean! See you at the Sugar Bowl!

Stingaroo! Stingarii! Stingaree!

Schroeder finished reading the story and turned **back** to Soapy and Petey. "What's this stingaroo stuff?"

Petey gestured toward Soapy. "That was his idea, **Mr.**

Schroeder. Soapy figured a little slogan would identify each one of Chip's supporters. He doped it out so a guy—er—senior, who was in on the deal—"

"What deal?"

"Well—er—the soda deal, sir. That is—er—Soapy and I figured you wouldn't mind taking all the free sodas and stuff out of our pay checks."

"That's why we had all the checks printed up, Mr. Schroeder," Soapy interrupted, "so you wouldn't be cheated."

"I can understand that," Schroeder said softly, "but what if Chip hadn't been elected?"

"Well, then, sir, the deal was off," Soapy explained. "The slips weren't any good if Chip wasn't elected and that's why we had so many seniors working for us and I guess one of the reasons we won. You see, when one of the seniors who had signed up with us, or rather promised us, his vote—"

Doc Jones coughed. "You mean a senior who had sold his vote to you for a soda slip, don't you?" he asked blandly.

"Yes—er, I guess that's right," Soapy agreed quickly. "Well, when one of those fellows met another senior he'd say 'stingaroo,' and if the other senior said 'stingarii,' the first one would come back with 'stingaree'!" Soapy looked proudly at Schroeder. "That was my idea! Clever, wasn't it?" he asked.

John Schroeder and Doc Jones eyed one another steadily for a long second. Then they turned back toward Soapy and nodded soberly. "Yes, that was extremely clever," they chorused.

Petey was worried. "I hope you can understand, Mr. Schroeder," he said anxiously, "Soapy and I meant to tell you all about it, but everything happened so fast we didn't have a chance. The whole amount comes to forty-five bucks—er—dollars."

"That's twenty-two and a half apiece, Mr. Schroeder," Soapy explained carefully. "You see, Petey and I went fifty-fifty on the proposition!"

John Schroeder nodded gravely and told the two worried youngsters he understood perfectly that one half of forty-five dollars, was twenty-two and a half apiece, but he couldn't understand their high and openhanded methods of conducting the soda fountain business of the Sugar Bowl. He further advised them that a repetition of the episode would find him prepared to send in a permanent substitute for each of them. Then he solemnly warned that he expected an accurate accounting of the soda slips and sent them back to their work. Soapy and Petey were strangely subdued the rest of that evening, but the other members of the Hilton A. C. were too happy and too busy to notice.

Chip still didn't understand it all, but he had learned enough of the coup to know that Zimmerman would be up in the air Thursday morning and that Chip Hilton would probably be in the soup again. He was absolutely correct. Right at that moment, the principal of Valley Falls High School *was* thinking about the election and Chip Hilton.

Supervising the voting tally, Zimmerman had discovered that afternoon just what the Big Red seniors had been up to and he was thoroughly enraged. William "Chip" Hilton, who led all the candidates with his write-in coup to a landslide victory, was most prominent in Zimmerman's thoughts. The Big Reds' baseball captain had drawn practically every vote. Zimmerman was also disturbed by the action of the editors of the *Yellow Jacket* in printing the story without authorization and he promised himself that he would use drastic measures on the morrow to curtail the activities of all concerned.

The next morning Chip felt as if he were sitting on a powder keg, but nothing happened. Right after lunch, however, Principal Zimmerman called an assembly and sternly announced that the election was illegal and that the results could not be accepted. A little later he called Chip to his office.

Chip stated he knew nothing about the election and, despite the principal's insistence, refused to divulge who had been responsible for the coup. Zimmerman tried his best to shake Chip in his stand, but the youngster could not be induced to talk. Finally, in desperation, the exasperated school head told Chip to go home and report back to his office next morning at nine o'clock.

As soon as Hilton left his office, Zimmerman sent for the editorial staff of the *Yellow Jacket*. The session was a stormy one. Before it was over many words were said that should have remained unsaid by a man in Zimmerman's position. Nancy Parker was an able editor and she stood her ground with considerable spunk. Chip Hilton was her hero. In the principal's actions she saw a deliberate course of persecution against Chip. She charged that the principal had presided over the election and that it had been a fair one. Before the interview was over everyone was talking at once, Zimmerman was shouting and Nancy Parker was in tears and threatening that her father, a successful lawyer, would bring action against the school board.

Baseball practice that afternoon was a farce. Chip did not report and Rockwell knew nothing about his suspension until Chet Stewart told him what had happened. Then the harassed coach appreciated the indifferent attitude of the Big Reds toward the workout. "That's all!" he barked. "Take three laps and hit the showers!"

Rockwell turned on his heel and hurried toward the gym, stamping his feet, swinging his arms, and muttering every step of the way. Through the dressing room, up the steel steps, past his office and down the hall, the angry coach stormed, unaware of the damage his spikes were inflicting on the highly polished floor. But Zimmerman's office was closed. Rockwell shook the door furiously, muttered something about "banker's hours," swung about, and stamped back down the hall.

Down at the Sugar Bowl that night, you would have thought the place had been sold. It was so quiet that the few customers who drifted in spoke in the low tones one expects to hear in a funeral parlor. Chip was buried in his books in the storeroom while Petey and Soapy were whispering excitedly, their heads close together at one end of the fountain. A little later they were joined by Speed Morris, Biggie Cohen, Red Schwartz, and every baseball regular. Right after the Sugar Bowl closed for the night, nine Big Red ballplayers and the manager of the team met at a prearranged rendezvous and then headed resolutely for the Zimmerman residence.

Lights were still burning in the house when Soapy boldly led the way up the steps and punched the doorbell. Zimmerman was sitting in the same chair he had occupied all during the bitter four-hour discussion with Henry Rockwell, still trying to justify his decision. But he knew the whole structure of his position was weak simply because he had let Mayor Condon influence his thinking and interfere with the administration of his job. The indignant coach had told him some things which he did not have the courage to admit to himself. Rockwell's parting words had cut him to the quick and he was still thinking about them. "Politics and education don't mix, Zimmerman," the veteran coach had said coolly just before he slammed the door.

Now, when the doorbell roused him, Zimmerman expressed his annoyance with a deep sigh and started for the door. When he saw his visitors, he knew instantly the purpose of their call and reluctantly escorted them to the living room. An embarrassed silence followed the entrance of the nine boys. But a few minutes later Petey had the floor and he began to tell the amazed educator all the details of the conversation he had overheard between Davis, Waters, Adams, and Weaver down at Sorelli's poolroom.

Then Soapy moved into action. "We'd have told you the whole story ten days ago," he said, "if Chip hadn't stopped us. Chip knew about it all along, but he said he'd handle it himself. We'd have let him do it, too, except for the election. Mr. Zimmerman, that election was on the level. The senior class elected Chip mayor and they don't understand the action you took this afternoon in calling it illegal and expelling Chip. If the election was illegal, then every senior who voted for Chip should be expelled from school. We have all the names of the fellows and girls who gave him their votes. You'll have to expel all of us or reinstate Chip."

Principal Zimmerman was a good man, if somewhat weak. He had, as Rockwell had said, failed to take a stand against the present city administration. One compromise had led to another, one appeasement to another. If he only had told Mayor Condon off at the very beginning, instead of allowing him to get his foot in the door. Rockwell would have stepped on that foot instead of opening the door. . . . His weakness in knuckling to Condon had cost him the respect of his school. His action toward Hilton had cost him his own self-respect.

But it still was not too late to take a stand. . . . As Petey and Soapy talked, he was studying the intense faces of what might well have been considered Valley Falls High School's inner athletic circle. What he saw in those earnest faces must have pleased him, and it must have done something to him, too, for he surprised his listeners, and himself, by abruptly rising, extending his hand to each in turn, and assuring them that the story they had brought threw a different light on the whole matter and that he proposed to do something about it.

The next afternoon at two o'clock the principal called a general assembly and it was a puzzled throng of whispering, wondering students who quickly filled the auditorium. Rumors had it that the staff of the *Yellow Jacket* would resign; that Chip Hilton would announce his resignation from the office to which he had been elected; and that there was to be another senior election that very afternoon. That was why no one was prepared for the principal's initial surprise, least of all, Chip Hilton.

After everyone was seated, Principal Zimmerman asked Chip to come forward. Chip, expecting further humiliation, made the platform some way, walking stiff-legged and feeling more self-conscious than he had ever felt in his life. As he passed Nancy Parker's seat on the side she whispered, "Heads up, Chip!" At the top of the short flight of steps Zimmerman surprised Chip again by grasping his hand and leading him to the center of the stage. Waiting for the whispering and foot-scraping to cease, the school head, looking calm and collected for the first time in days, smiled and then startled everyone by saying, "Members of the faculty and students of Valley Falls, I want to introduce you to the senior who will serve as the mayor of Valley Falls on Friday, June 18th."

There was a deep silence for what seemed a full minute before the import of the principal's words registered upon his listeners and then the room burst into applause with a roar as though an atom bomb had exploded. And its reverberations held most of those gathered there in a grip of joyous surprise long after the meeting had ended. Chip found his way to his seat in a daze. He never heard Zimmerman say that the entire staff of the *Yellow Jacket* had shown themselves to be true crusaders in the field of journalism.

Other candidates—their faces registering smug satisfaction as they entered the assembly room—were stunned and sat quietly in their seats when the others left.

Zimmerman and his staff of moderators had no chance to hold that assembly in check. Everyone was on his feet, cheering, and as if guided by an irresistible force, the whole gathering started moving; moving for the doors, spilling out of the exits and out of the building. There was no more school that day for the seniors of Valley Falls High School.

CHAPTER 10

THE BLOOPER PITCH

NICK TRULLO was in trouble. His arm had been aching ever since he had pivoted in the fifth and used Rockwell's pick-off play to catch a Dane runner off second base. The throw had been perfect, Speed Morris and Buzz Todd had played it right, and the runner had been out by a mile. But the twinge in Trullo's arm had changed to an ache in the sixth and, in the seventh, the pain in his deltoid muscle was continuous and intense. Trullo finished it out, but he sat quietly in the dugout holding his upper left arm tightly with his big right hand through the top of the eighth.

The arm was as tight as a drum, and when he walked out to the mound in the bottom of the frame to take his warm-up throws, the wing felt as though he were swinging a piece of wood.

Rockwell had been trying every trick in the bag in an effort to overcome the Dane lead, but here it was the bottom of the eighth and the run Dane had scored in the third was getting bigger and bigger. To make it worse, the Big Reds' bats had been silenced completely by Dane's strike-out king, Bullet Nichols. Rockwell had kept Chip on the bench hoping to rest him up for Steeltown and planning to use his star hurler as a pinch hitter if a break came. But the Big Reds couldn't get to first base. This was a "must" game. Valley Falls had to win this one or else forget about the state tournament. So far as that was concerned, all three games with Dane, Steeltown, and Salem, were "must" games.

Chip had been rooting on every pitch and on every play. Now, he sent a barrage of cheering words in Nick's direction. Then he noticed there was something wrong with Trullo's delivery. Before he could bring it to Rockwell's attention, the Dane hitters had pounced on Nick's nothing ball and runners were perched on first and second with none away.

"Coach," Chip cried, "Trullo's arm's gone! I noticed it in his warm-up!"

But Rockwell was already on his way. "Time!" he called. "Time!"

Nick Trullo was no quitter. Every throw he had made in the last two frames had been followed by a blast of fire which began just below his elbow and raced up his arm and through his shoulder. But he hadn't said a word; had tried to conceal the pain. The big southpaw wanted to win this one on his own so Chip would be ready for the big game with Steeltown four days away. Then he could take his turn against Salem three days after that and they might be able to come through. But now, as Rockwell came striding toward him, Nick knew he had gone as far as he could; he had nothing left.

Rockwell needed only one sharp glance at Trullo's tense face to realize that the boy was in pain. The harried mentor glanced out in right field toward Soapy Smith, pondered a second as he caught Chip's eye in the dugout, and then beckoned for Soapy. Then, placing an arm around Trullo's shoulders, Rockwell gently led the boy off the field.

Chip was on his feet and out of the dugout just as Rockwell signaled Soapy. And before Trullo and the coach had taken five steps he was beside them. Chip grasped Trullo's hand affectionately and looked understandingly into his eyes. "Too bad, Nick," he said sympathetically, "don't worry about it!" Ignoring Rockwell's restraining hand, Chip turned toward the mound, waved Soapy back to right field, and motioned for Carl Carey to throw him the ball.

"Atta boy, Chip!"

"Mow 'em down, Chipper!"

"Down the old alley, kid!"

But Chip didn't throw them down the alley. He shook Carl Carey off until he got the right sign and then placed four pitches just out of the reach of the hitter to fill the bases. Then he took a deep breath. Now the play was at any base.

It was good baseball and it paid off. The hitter was too anxious; went after a fast one around his knees and pulled a hard, single-bounce ball right at Chuck Badger. Chuck fielded it flawlessly, stepped on third, and nearly tore Tuffy Collins' glove off with his throw to second. So now there were two away and a runner on first.

Chip had been sizing up the Dane hitters all through the game and he had tabbed the batter facing him with a gun-shy label. He liked to sidearm a righty when the fellow didn't like them close. This hitter didn't like them close and was called out with his bat on his shoulder.

Rockwell met them in front of the dugout as they came trotting in. "Now, let's go get a couple of runs," he urged. "Come on! Last licks! Got to be!"

It didn't look good and, in his heart, Chip knew it. But he pepped it up with the rest of them. Lefty Peters, up at the plate, couldn't hit the size of his hat, and Carl Carey, on deck, was almost as bad. But a fellow had to stick with his teammates; good or bad he had to make them feel they could do it.

He kept chirping away as he hefted two bats and mentally timed his swing with Bullet Nichols' fast ball. The big righty had lost none of his speed and every pitch seemed to have a hop on it, but Chip wasn't worried. He liked the swift pitch.

Lefty Peters wasn't any bigger than a minute as he stood up there, determined to follow Rockwell's orders.

"Make him pitch, Lefty. Make him pitch!"

"Get on, Lefty. We'll bring you in!"

Nichols fogged them in, but Lefty didn't give an inch. He just stood there, crowding the plate; looking no bigger than little Paddy Jackson. And he worked the count to two and one.

"Brush him back, Bullet! Brush him back!"

"Stay up there, Lefty! Look 'em over!"

"Get on, Lefty! Chip'll bring you in! *You* get on!"

Lefty dug in and crowded the plate and that got Nichols' goat. He wasn't the kind of pitcher a hitter took liberties with; didn't like batters who took a toe hold. The fast one streaked in, but it was too close and too fast and it caught Lefty smack in his ribs. The ball thudded in with a vicious thump and Lefty dropped. But there was a grim smile on his lips as he clambered to his feet, brushed off his teammates hands, and trotted down to first. Lefty was on!

Chip moved into the circle, knelt down, and watched Nichols intently. It was this inning and no other inning. Now or never. The whole season depended upon scoring at least one run. And it was going to be right up to him no matter what happened to Lefty and Carl. He looked at the right-field fence and then gave himself a mental kick in the pants. Babe Ruth could point to a fence and deliver . . . but he was no Babe Ruth. . . . He'd concentrate on meeting the ball.

Carey took a called strike across the letters, turned up his nose at a low one outside, and then sent Lefty scampering to second on a fast-rolling bunt down the first-base line which the first baseman handled too late to make a play at second and barely in time to beat Carl to first. So there, in answer to the Big Reds' frantic pleas, was the duck on the pond. And it was up to Chip Hilton to get it home.

Chip took his time getting around to the first-base side of the batter's box, tugging his cap, pulling at his belt, wiping first the right hand and then the left hand across the front of his shirt, tapping his left shoe with the bat and then the right; but at last he was there and he dug in, got himself a good toe hold. One brief glance sufficed to place the positions of the Dane outfielders. They had shifted far toward the right.

Bullet Nichols knew Chip Hilton and so did the fans. Every Dane rooter there remembered one or more football, basketball, or baseball games which the tall, slender youngster at the plate had broken up, and they decided to give him the works. They didn't think he could do it, yet you couldn't tell about this kid. Anyway, they'd give him all they had; maybe it would help. They came up on their feet with a roar of derision and taunts. Nichols did his part, too. Hilton was a power hitter and ballplayers who hit the long ball don't like to get all set and then be kept waiting. So Nichols fiddled around, smoothed out a little pile of dirt behind the mound, looked and faked at Lefty on second, and fiddled and fooled until the umpire behind the plate got nervous and barked, "Play ball!"

Chip stood in the batter's box, completely relaxed,

bat resting on the plate. Then, when Nichols toed the rubber, Chip stepped back out of the box. The umpire glared at Chip and raised his hands. "Now what's the matter with *you?*" he growled. "Come on, play ball."

Chip laughed and waited until Nichols stepped back off the mound. Then he went through his batting ritual again and stepped up to the platter. Nichols didn't fiddle now. He took his stretch, and threw a duster which came in like a streak of lightning, and he laughed delightedly when Chip avoided the speeding ball only by dropping flat on his face. Chip got up slowly, picked up his cap, looked questioningly at the umpire as he dusted himself off, and then stepped back in the box.

Nichols came in then with an overhand slider which broke across Chip's belt and evened the count at one and one. He followed that with a change-up curve which fooled Chip for the one-and-two call and Nichols was out in front. Nichols fired his fast one inside then, and it evened up the count once more. Right then, Chip decided he'd go for the next one; he wouldn't wait for the full count.

It was the big righty's slider, and, although Chip's bat was late, it proved to be just the ticket. There was a sharp crack and the ball took off in a screaming line over the shortstop's head, past the left fielder, clear to the fence. Lefty was away with the hit and scored as Chip drove toward second. Then, the Dane left fielder made a mistake; he threw to the keystone sack. Chip couldn't believe it, but took advantage of the miscue, turning on the speed and heading for third. It was close, but he beat the relay by an eyelash, sliding safely under the throw from the second sacker.

Chip got up slowly then, and took his first real deep breath. A quick glance at the scoreboard reassured him; it was all tied up! The Big Reds were back in the ball game! He glanced at Chet Stewart in the first-base coaching box and then at Collins. The little second sacker was receiving last-minute instructions from Rockwell and tapping his bat aggressively on the red clay. A second later he was up at the plate and Chip got the sign from Stewart. The squeeze was on, but Tuffy was on his own with respect to the pitch he'd choose. That put Chip on the spot, too, for the Dane infield was in tight, determined to cut him off at the plate.

Tuffy brought the crowd to its feet as he dumped a perfect roller down the first-base line and chased it so closely he had to swerve out of the base path to avoid the rushing first baseman. Chip slid in under the throw to put the Big Reds ahead by a score of 2 to 1 and Tuffy was safe at first.

Chip was up on his feet before the umpire roared "Safe!" only to be knocked down again by his charging teammates who mobbed him all the way to the dugout.

Tuffy Collins died on first on Speed's pop-up to the catcher and the Big Reds hustled out on the field for the bottom of the ninth with a one-run lead. Chip was still a bit breathless and took his time getting out to the mound. But the 2–1 score looked big now. Speed Morris helped out by stabbing a grasscutter far to his right and making the long throw like a big-leaguer, to catch the runner by a step for the first out. The second hitter banged a vicious line drive right back to Chip who couldn't get out of the way and didn't even know how he caught the speeding ball. But it brought a big cheer from the stands and two were away.

That brought the game down to that famous "last man." It was the Dane center gardener and cleanup hitter. Every Dane rooter was on his feet yelling for "Pete" to hit it out of the park. He nearly did it, too. He caught Chip's fast ball flush on the nose, but pulled it foul. That gave Chip a scare and warned him that "Pete" liked the hard one. So Chip's change-up came twirling in for the second strike and he was out in front. Then Chip fired a blazing fast one high outside, but Pete watched it go by without moving his bat.

Standing there, ball hand and arm dangling behind him, Chip thought of something. Why not try the blooper? . . . He had used it but once all year. . . .

He shook Carey off until Carl finally remembered. Chip nodded, wound up, gripped the ball with his fingernails and pulled the string. The ball shot up and out and, after what seemed an hour, floated lazily down toward the plate, big as a balloon. "Pete" watched the ball coming straight down in the strike zone and then swung so mightily that he twisted clear around like a top and fell to the ground. And he was still sitting there looking for the hole in his bat after Carl Carey had tucked that third-strike ball in his pocket and headed for the Valley Falls dugout.

Mary Hilton had scanned her son's face intently the night before and noted the fatigue in the troubled gray eyes. That was the reason she had moved so quietly about the house this Sunday morning. It was nine thirty when Chip finally appeared in the kitchen and gave his mother a good-morning kiss.

"Sorry, Mother," he said sheepishly, "I just died. I couldn't get up."

"You needed the rest, Chip," Mrs. Hilton said softly, smoothing back the boy's unruly blond hair. "You look much better this morning. Feel better, too, don't you?"

Chip's answer was to give Mary Hilton what they called his "carrousel whirl." Before she could move he lifted her high in the air and swung her around and around until she was gasping for breath. Then he lowered her tenderly and kissed her again. "What do you think?" he asked gaily.

"I think you had *too* much rest," she responded. "Now, you just sit down there and behave yourself!"

After breakfast Chip delved into the sports pages of the Sunday newspapers. Pete Williams lauded Chip's hitting and relief pitching, but not Muddy Waters.

TIMES AND SPORTS

BY MUDDY WATERS

Valley Falls won a game yesterday afternoon, defeating Dane High School and the great Bullet Nichols by a score of 2 to 1 . . . But . . . The Big Reds lost Nick Trullo because of overwork and one more black mark can be chalked up against the bleacher slugger.

Trullo was forced to carry the whole load during Hilton's suspension and the overwork strained his arm. . . . Coach Henry Rockwell kept Trullo in the game inning after inning when it was apparent to this observer that the big southpaw was pitching solely with his heart.

Rockwell was undoubtedly saving Hilton for Steeltown. . . . Is the Steeltown game that important? . . . Important enough to risk ruining a kid's arm? . . . Why does Rockwell persist in protecting Hilton at the expense of the other members of the team?

Chalk up yesterday's win to stellar fielding by the Big Reds and to little Lefty Peters' cleverness in working Bullet Nichols for a pass which led to the tying run.

Tuffy Collins was the real star thanks to his clutch squeeze bunt which scored Hilton with the winning run.

Steeltown is in . . . so far as Section Two is concerned . . . The Iron Men now have a record of 10 and 3 with two to go . . . The Big Reds here next Wednesday, June 16, and Southern at Steeltown on Saturday, June 19. The Steelers should win both games with not too much trouble, from where we sit.

Valley Falls now has a record of nine and four . . . The Big Reds and the Sailors both have two to go and meet head on at Salem, June 19. . . .

There was a breath-slowing tightness in Chip's chest when he finished the write-up. He sighed deeply and shook his head questioningly. What in the world was Waters trying to do?

Minutes later he turned to the front page of the *Times*. There was the usual world news features which he read quickly and then his eyes ranged over the page and came to a sudden stop.

"No!" he muttered. "What's this—"

MUDDLED HIGH SCHOOL POLITICS

*Traditional Senior Election Is Farce
Cheapened by Vote Sales*

BY MUDDY WATERS

The annual senior election to determine the student administrators of Valley Falls on Friday, June 18, was held last Wednesday. And for the first time in the history of this traditional activity, the election was a farce.

This reporter learned from reliable sources that the majority of the voters supporting the write-in candidates sold out for cheap refreshment promises payable at John Schroeder's Sugar Bowl.

That the school authorities will countenance this travesty of an important civic activity is inconceivable; that the young men and women who will be graduated from our high school in less than two weeks would regard their responsibilities so lightly is incomprehensible.

In former years, the seriousness and sincerity accompanying the election made this extracurricular activity one of the most important events on the senior calendar. A number of Valley Falls' leading citizens have voiced deep concern in the matter and drastic action can be expected in the next few days.

William "Chip" Hilton, who was suspended from school two weeks ago for attacking a spectator at one of the baseball games, was the successful write-in candidate. It is difficult to believe that such strong-arm methods will be countenanced in school politics irrespective of the importance of the group to the school's athletic program.

Chip was dismayed. "Well, what do you think of that?" he said aloud. "Why, that—"

"Are you talking to me, Chip?" his mother called from the kitchen.

"No, Mother," Chip answered, folding the paper hastily. "Just talking to myself."

Just about that time in a small house perched high on the hill on the South Side, Buck Adams and Peck Weaver were gloating over Muddy Waters' column and the news it contained.

"Pours it on, that Waters," Weaver chuckled.

"Yeah," Adams agreed, "And now everything's just right. Trullo's out and that means all we hafta do is get Hilton. Then we'll have Rockwell where we want him."

"We better work fast," Weaver warned. "They've only got two more games, and Hilton's good! He could beat Steeltown and Salem both, all by himself! That would give 'em a record of eleven and four, put 'em in the play-offs for the state!"

"Yeah," Adams agreed, "let's see. Steeltown's ten and three now. If Hilton beats 'em Wednesday, that would tie the two of them up. Who the Steelers play next?"

"Southern at Southern," Weaver breathed, "and those Tarheels are tough!"

Adams nodded his head decisively. "Yep," he said, "you're right! We gotta move fast! We'll get Hilton Wednesday afternoon!"

CHAPTER 11

MISS VALLEY FALLS

"It says here," Soapy said ponderously, reading from the time-yellowed pages of a copy of Valley Falls' city ordinances, year 1850, "that every resident of Valley Falls must stand still when the clock strikes three o'clock to com—er, commensurate the erection of the dam above the city in 1845."

"Commemorate," Biggie growled.

"Well, then, commemorate," Soapy said defiantly. "What's the diff? Commensurate or commemorate, it's all commerce!"

That brought a hail of protest from everyone and the purpose of the meeting was forgotten as Soapy caught it from all sides. Upstairs, in the living room over Chip's laboratory in the basement, Mary Hilton smiled and glanced at the clock on the mantel. This particular Sunday afternoon meeting of the Hilton A. C. was evidently an important one. The boys had been in noisy session nearly two hours.

It was important all right. Important to Chip's plans for the following Friday and he let those present understand it in no uncertain terms. "Come on, now," he said firmly, "we're wasting time. Let Soapy finish! But remember, we've got lots to do between now and Friday. Go ahead, Soapy—"

"Okay," Soapy said in an aggrieved tone. "I'm ready. Hey, here's a good one. Peanuts must be eaten in the store in which they are purchased. Furthermore, it is illegal to stand more than five minutes in any one place.

"Lollipops may not be sold between the hours of eight A.M. and five P.M."

Soapy chuckled. "Oh, boy, this'll ruin old man Thomas. It says here that a man may not wear a goatee unless he pays a fee or a tax.

"Here's a peach! It's against the law in Valley Falls to sell beer unless the tavern has a kettle of soup brewing. Would you—er—say Mike Sorelli's in the soup? Ha!"

Soapy let out a hoot of laughter. "Oh, boy! Listen to this! No person in Valley Falls may give his sweetheart a box of candy weighing less than five pounds. Wait'll the boss gets a load of that!"

A few minutes later Soapy finished reading the list of laws his department had selected to be enforced on June 18th. Then Chip took over.

"Now here's the list of offices. Write them down. Biggie, you'll serve as chief of police, and judging from the number of laws you'll have to enforce, you're going to need about fifty special officers. Taps' mother made fifty arm bands and it's up to you to select a good force. You're going to be busy!

"Nick, you'll be the sheriff and you'll need some deputies. And Tuffy and Chuck and Red will be regular cops. Speed, you'll take Judge Graham's place; Lefty will be city engineer—

"Soapy, you'll be chief of detectives and it's up to you to choose your own staff. Taps, you'll be the fire chief.

Carl, you'll be auditor. Here's a list of the other officers."

"What about these girls here?" Carl Carey asked doubtfully, looking at the list of names. "You mean we *have* to put up with them?"

Soapy chortled with glee. "Look who's kicking," he said boisterously. "The great lover's protesting! Huh!"

"We've *got* to put up with them," Chip said patiently. "Mr. Zimmerman made the selections. Nancy Parker is council secretary—"

"Ain't gonna be no female flatfoots on my force," Soapy growled. "Hey," he said brightly, "who's your secretary, or is that question too personal?"

"Er, no," Chip said hesitantly. "Mr. Zimmerman appointed Kathryn Gibson—"

"KATHRYN GIBSON!"

"The cover girl?"

"Miss *Valley Falls*?"

"Gentlemen prefer blondes!"

"Take a letter, Kathryn, dear!"

"Yoo-hoo! Yoo-hoo, Mayor!"

Chip finally got them quieted. "Well, I guess that's it," he said crisply.

The principal of Valley Falls High School expected a call from Mayor Condon the first thing Monday morning, and he wasn't disappointed. The call came exactly at 9:05 A.M. and Zimmerman's voice was precise and steady when he answered.

"Yes, Mr. Condon. Fine! . . . Oh, the election. Yes, that's all settled. . . . The paper *was* right, Mayor; the Hilton boy *was* elected. . . . Why, yes, Mr. Condon, the boy was elected fairly, practically by a unanimous vote. . . . But write-in voting *is* legal, Mayor. . . .

"I'm sorry, sir, but I can't do that! . . . No, the boy was elected and the matter is closed. In fact, all of the offices are filled and can't be changed. . . . I'm sorry you feel that way, Mayor, but there's nothing I can do—Good-bye, sir!"

Zimmerman's face was set in grim lines when he cradled the receiver and leaned back in his chair. Well, that was that! He'd better get busy on that new job! He had a hunch Valley Falls would be a memory, come September.

Around the horn and back to Cohen, that's the way the Big Reds hustled the ball around the infield. And that's the way they zipped it around when they took the field Wednesday afternoon. Biggie always handled the ball last; before it went to the pitcher. Now, as he palmed and twisted the game-ball, trying to remove some of its shiny newness, he walked close to Chip.

"This is a big one, Chipper; bear down all the way. They're good and they beat us before, remember?"

Chip remembered. The Steelers had beaten Trullo 3 to 2 earlier in the season to give the Big Reds their first setback. He hadn't forgotten that and he wasn't going to forget that this was a *must* win. If Valley Falls lost today, they would be completely out of the race and Steeltown could be sure of the runner-up spot, maybe the championship. Yes, this was a must win. And it was all up to him. Today and Saturday, too . . . Nick would be out for at least two weeks . . . Maybe for the play-off games at State . . . If . . .

The Valley Falls–Steeltown sports rivalry was as keen as constant pressure could make it. Year after year the high school teams representing these two rival towns were among the leaders in the state, and usually figured in the stretch race for Section Two honors. This year Steeltown had one of its best teams in years and the early-season win over the Big Reds at Steeltown had given them confidence, made them cocky. The Big Reds' fans noticed the visitors' cockiness right off the bat, and when the state champs trotted out on the field to start the game, they were surprised by the intensity of the crowd-roar of support.

Back of Chip, his teammates were pepping it up, confident of his ability to take the Steelers. It was great to play on a team with that kind of spirit and Chip swallowed hard to get rid of the choked feeling in his throat. Then he toed the rubber, took Soapy's sign, and everything was forgotten except the batter at the plate.

"Break their backs, Chipper," Soapy bellowed, "give it to me, baby! Down the old alley! Gimme that apple!"

Chip felt relaxed and right. His fast one had a hop on it and his change-up curve was finding the corners. He got the big end of the Steelers' batting order one, two, three. But Bob Lennox was just as good, equaling Chip's performance. Lennox was a master of the soft stuff, tantalizing curves and the slow, twisting knuckler. And today his control was perfect.

That's the way it went for three innings, each pitcher matching the other. So far, both hurlers were pitching perfect ball. Neither had been touched for a single bingle. Chip kept the pace in the top of the fourth, holding the Iron Men helpless. With the last out, he was greeted by a roar of approval from the stands. As he walked across the limed first-base line, he lifted a hand to touch the bill of his cap in response to the applause. Then he saw Adams and Weaver. They were sitting right back of the Big Reds' dugout, eyes mean and angry, glaring straight at him. Some presentiment warned Chip. They were planning something; they had been altogether too quiet. . . .

Chip continued on to the dugout without another glance at the stands. Then it happened! Each time the Big Reds came in from the field, Adams had watched for an opportunity to pull the trick he and Weaver had planned. A quick glance around decided him that this was the time. Two fellows seated beside Adams stood up and leaned over him briefly, concealing the heckler from view. Buck leaned forward, over the top of the dugout, and spat a full mouth of tobacco juice straight into the unsuspecting chucker's face.

Chip had expected something, but Adams and Weaver had been so quiet that he was completely surprised by the sudden action. Without thinking, he changed direction and charged around the dugout, heading for the bleachers and Buck Adams. Then, just as he placed his hands on the railing in front of the first row of seats, he stopped short, suddenly conscious of what he was doing; aware that his involuntary reaction was leading him straight into another trap. He stood there for a second, then clamped his jaws to still the angry words rushing through his mind, and turned away. He was still wiping the tobacco juice from his eyes when he ducked under the sheltering roof of the dugout.

The incident passed unnoticed by the spectators and Chip's teammates, but Rockwell had seen what had happened. He leaped out of the dugout, hoping to be in time to stop Chip from reaching his tormentors. But Chip was on his way back from the fence and never saw Rockwell. But both heard the derisive laughter of Adams and Weaver and a burning flame of anger almost got the best of each of them.

Chip wasn't the only one finding it difficult to bring himself under control. Rockwell, too, had just about reached the end of the string with respect to Adams and Weaver. Perhaps it was fortunate for everyone concerned that Speed Morris stopped on the way to the bat rack at that moment for instructions.

"Shall I wait him out, Coach?" Speed asked.

"Er, yes, let's try it, Speed," Rockwell said uncertainly, "you've got a good eye; make him put it in there."

Speed worked Lennox for the first walk of the game and the hopeful roar of the home crowd drowned out the abuse Adams and Weaver were hurling at Rockwell and Hilton.

The pass Speed Morris had drawn was the first break for the Big Reds, and Rockwell forced himself to concentrate on the game. Red Schwartz followed orders, and his sacrifice bunt put Speed on second with Biggie Cohen up at the plate. The big southpaw had a good eye, and he worked Lennox for the full count. Then Biggie smacked a slow curve in the hole between right and center for two bases, and Speed trotted across the plate with the first run of the game. Lennox really went to work then, setting Chuck Badger down with two smoke balls and a change-up curve in three fast pitches, and his soft stuff had Soapy Smith swinging from his heels and out with a pop-up to the catcher.

The excitement aroused by the short flare of action and the first score of the game gave Chip a chance to calm his anger. But he was still jumpy when he walked out to the hill for the top of the fifth. He tried to forget the incident, concentrated on Soapy's target and poured his warm-up pitches through the strike zone. But it wasn't easy. The South Side contingent wasn't going to let him forget.

"What's the matter, grandstander? Can't you take it?"

"Rockwell's pet's peeved!"

"Yeah, the act flopped! Couldn't work his bluff today!"

"Boo, Hilton, boo!"

The Steelers didn't know what it was all about and

the rooters behind their dugout didn't get it either, but they were quick to pick it up. Soon, supporting cheers of the loyal Valley Falls rooters were drowned out by the shouts leveled at the Big Reds' star hurler.

Despite Chip's resolve to ignore the crowd, it was impossible. His fast ball streaked in, but he was aiming too carefully at Soapy's target and his control faltered. The burning anger returned and he put too much on the ball, tried too hard, and the result was the loss of just a bit more of his control. The first two pitches barely missed the corners for the count of two and no, and the Steeler taunts came rolling out to the mound in an ever-increasing crescendo.

Baseball fans possess almost incredible powers in sensing the emotional instability of a pitcher and these rabid rooters knew Chip Hilton by heart; knew when he was right and when he was upset. And they had him figured correctly now, for the batter drew four straight balls for Chip's first walk of the game. And in spite of Soapy's delaying tactics, Chip walked the second hitter also. Rockwell called time then and walked slowly out to the mound. There he was joined in the huddle by Soapy, Biggie, Speed, Tuffy, and Chuck as the fans whooped it up. The mingled roar of support, gibes, and catcalls reverberated through the grounds around the little group, drowning out all hopes of normal speaking, and Rockwell was almost shouting as he addressed Chip.

"Forget it, kid. Don't fall for the trick. You're too smart! Don't let them get your goat with a little bit of razzing."

Biggie threw a heavy arm around Chip's shoulders, gripping his friend's arm with a hamlike hand. "Come on, Chip," he cried, "remember what this game means— We're behind you. Push 'em in there. Let 'em hit!"

Rockwell's black eyes were focused intently on Chip's

face, and when the boy nodded and thumped the ball into his glove, the veteran coach knew the crisis had passed. Four long years of training and observation had endowed Rockwell with a complete understanding of Chip Hilton. He took the ball from the glove, tossed it to Biggie, and leaned close to Chip. "Walk the next hitter, boy," he said loudly, "then go to work!"

Four away-from-the-plate throws and the bases were loaded. Every fan in the park was on his feet, yelling at the top of his voice, and the taunts of the South Siders were lost in the din. Chip wouldn't have heard them anyway. Once again he was the kid chucker from Valley Falls who rated number one in the state.

Chip eyed the batter, crowding the plate, obviously up there to wait him out. The base runners danced on the base paths, daring a throw, but Chip wasn't interested. He shook Soapy off until he got the sign for the fast one, inside, around the belt. And he flashed two of them "in there" for a nothing-and-two count which moved the batter back from the plate. Then he pulled the string on a change-up twister and the Steeler broke his back, missing the ball by a country mile.

The next hitter was tall and rawboned. He had power written all over him, from the high-held bat to the full-stride stance. Chip noted the away-from-body elbows and the steady bat. Here was a pull hitter, a clutch hitter . . . Maybe he'd go for a fast outside-corner pitch . . . The Iron Man went for it, reaching out with his bat instead of stepping into the ball, and Chip was ahead, "nothing and one."

Soapy called for a change-up, but Chip's keen gray eyes had noted the short stance the Steeler had assumed. The hitter didn't seem comfortable up there, and Chip figured the slugger was guessing with him; was looking for a twister. So he waited for Soapy to call for the fast one and then sent the ball zipping right in where the big boy liked them, right across the letters, in close. It was a perfect pitch for a pull hitter, but the batter wasn't ready and realized his mistake too late. His hasty forward stride dipped his bat a bit, but he still got a piece of the hopping ball, sending a lazy liner to short right center. Schwartz played the pitch like a big-leaguer, raced in on a dead run, snared the ball from his shoelaces, and pegged a perfect strike to Soapy.

The Steeler on third had been fooled by the blow, figuring at first it would drop in front of Schwartz for a hit. So he started for home, only to reverse to tag-up, when the frantic third-base coach chased him and he saw his teammates waving him back. Then, when Schwartz caught the ball, he lost his head completely, threw caution to the winds, and raced for home, determined to force a play at the plate. He didn't have a chance. Soapy charged gleefully up the base path and met the runner head-on, meat hand gripping the ball like a vise in the pocket of his glove, and he was still holding the precious pill when he somersaulted to his feet and tossed it to the umpire.

Chip yelped thankfully at Soapy and turned to grab Schwartz by the hand as the redhead came trotting into the dugout. He didn't know what he said and Red didn't either. But it didn't matter, for the thundering roar from the stands drowned out his words and those of everyone else.

The Big Reds couldn't score in the bottom of that hectic inning, but it wasn't important. Chip held the Steelers scoreless all the rest of the way and the Big Reds didn't need their bottom-of-the-ninth turn at bat.

Going home in Speed's jalopy, pleasantly relaxed, Chip was oblivious to the boisterous yells of Soapy and Red. He was replaying the game and thinking of the near run-in with Adams and Weaver. Thoughts of Adams and Weaver brought a grim smile to his lips. He hadn't fallen into their trap this time and he wasn't going to fall the next time . . . Guess the win this afternoon had surprised everyone. Valley Falls and Steeltown were tied for second place now, each with identical records of 10 and 4. . . .

Salem was sure of the championship. The Sailors had won fourteen and lost only one. He wasn't going to forget that game or the duel with Kip Parcels for a long time. Parcels was good! Anyway, the Big Reds had won that one just as they had won today and by the same score. Maybe he could beat Parcels again. It would be up to him all right. Nick's arm was still bad. . . .

Just suppose the Big Reds beat Salem and Southern's kids trimmed Steeltown. That would put Valley Falls in the play-offs! And anything could happen if a team got to the tournament. Valley Falls had come in second in Section Two once before and had gone up to State and won the championship. Maybe they could do it again. It was a crazy thought, all right, but lots of crazy things happened in baseball. They'd be in a tough situation, though, if they won the runner-up spot. What would the Rock do for another chucker? Well, anyway, they had a chance. Wishful thinking maybe, but you couldn't blame a fellow for dreaming. And trying. . . .

CHAPTER 12

MAYOR FOR A DAY

"HIYA, MAYOR! How's things down at City Hall?"

"Yeah, Mayor, when you gonna clean up the joint?"

"Going to put a new sidewalk in front of your house?"

"When you goin' fishing, Mayor? How about a ride?"

Chip smiled and hurried back to the storeroom. All morning at school the big topic of the day had been the important victory over the Steelers. But when the cafeteria opened its doors at lunchtime, the game was passé and the morrow's administration of Valley Falls by the senior class held everyone's attention. And during the rest of the day at school and at baseball practice Chip had heard little else. Now, at the Sugar Bowl, he was busy in the storeroom with his plans. But he took time to read the story in the *Post*.

HIGH SCHOOL SENIORS TAKE OVER
CITY GOVERNMENT

William Hilton Mayor-for-a-Day

Tomorrow is the day for the Valley Falls seniors who were elected or appointed to fill city offices for a day. The students will report to their respective offices bright and early tomorrow morning to get acquainted with their duties. The complete list of officers follows:

Mayor: William Hilton

Secretary: Kathryn Gibson

City Council: Robert Parsons, president; Nancy Parker, secretary; William Single; James Cooper; Arnold West

City Judge: Robert Morris

City Engineer: Fred Peters

Sheriff: Nicholas Trullo

Chief of Police: Bernie Cohen

Patrolmen: Edward Schwartz; Theodore Collins; Charles Badger

Chief of Detectives: Robert Smith

Fire Chief: George Browning

Auditor: Carl Carey

Chip was breathing fast when he finished reading the paper and checking the names of his staff. For a moment he was disturbed as he thought of the reaction which was sure to follow the execution of his carefully laid plans. But that feeling persisted for a second only. Chip knew he was right and as things stood there wasn't much he could do about it now. It was too late to change his course of action.

Chip and the seniors who made up the City Council reported to the mayor's office the following morning at nine o'clock. Photographers from the *Post*, the *Times*, and the *Yellow Jacket* were on hand. They smiled cheerfully when they spoke to Chip and the council members, but they were quite serious about the pictures.

"Hold it, Mayor! Just a minute now!"

"That's it! Move a little to the left, Miss, er, Gibson—"

"Chip, look right at your secretary— Oh, boy!"

Chip glared at Orndorff and resolved to discuss certain things with the *Yellow Jacket* columnist at the first opportunity.

After the publicity ceremonies were finished, Mayor Condon escorted Chip and his classmates to the town's executive offices and left them with a pleasant "good morning and good luck!"

Chip walked gingerly around Condon's desk and seated himself in the big leather chair. "This is something," he said slowly, softly rubbing his hands across the top of the polished mahogany.

"Push all those buttons and see what happens," Red Schwartz urged, pointing to the interoffice communication box. "Let's start something!"

Chip checked him. "Never mind that," he said firmly, "we've already started something. First thing on the program is a meeting of the council."

In the council room, Chip reviewed the day's plans and received a unanimous vote of confidence.

"That settles it," he said quietly, "we'll proceed according to plan, beginning at two o'clock this afternoon. Don't forget now," he warned, "the baseball team's got to be at practice at three thirty. We've got to beat Salem tomorrow, and that means all the alternates will move up to their jobs after the team leaves for practice." He turned to Robert Parsons. "You'll be acting mayor, Bob, and it's up to you to follow through."

At twelve o'clock Mayor Condon appeared to escort Chip and the council members to the Chamber of Commerce luncheon at Valley Hotel. It was the biggest turnout of the year. It seemed to Chip that every important person in town was in the milling throng. As he and his council members were led to places at the head table, once again his heart jumped as he scanned the smiling faces of the men and his classmates who were seated at the various tables. A lot of these leading citizens were in for a big surprise before *this* day was over.

After the luncheon there were several brief speeches and then Mayor Condon was introduced. He spoke glowingly about the enthusiasm shown by the seniors and predicted great futures for "these fine young men and women." Then Condon introduced "our new mayor," and it took all of Chip's will power to master his feelings. But he made it and, as the representative of his classmates, thanked Mayor Condon, the Chamber of Commerce, and the citizens of Valley Falls for their kindness and thoughtfulness in giving his class the opportunity to learn so much about city government.

Mayor Hilton found it extremely difficult to shorten the after-luncheon pleasantries and humorous references with which the members of the Chamber of Commerce assailed him. But he tactfully explained that he was plagued with a lot of serious city problems and that some of them were dynamite.

"You never know when the fireworks are going to cut loose when you hold public office," he said meaningly.

Half an hour later, one would have thought that the Valley Falls High School student body was picketing the mayor's office. Practically every senior, boy and girl, was on hand. By two o'clock, the mimeographed plans which had been worked out by the inner circle were distributed. Then the dynamite, to which "Mayor Hilton" had referred, exploded.

Two hours later the members of the Valley Falls baseball team trotted out on Ohlsen Field chuckling and laughing and imbued with more spirit than Rockwell had seen all year. But he didn't waste time wondering about it, simply chalked it up to the lift of the Steeltown victory, hustled them through a fast workout, off to the showers and home for their suitcases.

"Bus leaves at six o'clock sharp," he admonished. "Be on time! I want to get to Salem by eleven o'clock! We'll eat at Weston—"

The bus pulled out at six o'clock sharp, all right, followed by the strains of the Big Reds' victory march. Every member of the hundred-piece band was on hand to give the team a real send-off.

"Might think we were off for the state tournament," Schwartz remarked.

Soapy snorted. "Give us time, pal," he chided. "This time next Tuesday we'll be on our way. Right, gang?"

The affirmative roar which greeted the question was music to Rockwell's ears. He sighed contentedly. This team was up! Way up! He leaned back in his seat, closed his eyes, and relaxed. It had been a slow day. He had missed the seniors around school and nothing much had happened in his office.

Henry Rockwell would have been surprised had he been able to hear certain conversations back in Valley Falls. He would have been amazed, too, to hear that the past afternoon had been one of the most event-packed in the town's history and that some persons were holding him responsible. At that very moment, in fact, Jerry Davis was sitting in Mayor Condon's office talking about the Big Reds' coach.

"Rockwell's behind this whole affair, Mayor. I'll bet he planned it!"

Condon nodded. "I wouldn't be surprised," he said bitterly. "He's always backed up that Hilton kid. I never heard of such a thing."

"Well, why don't you do something about it? Why

don't you get the board to retire him? Right now! Ohl-sen's out of town and you'd have a majority."

Condon slowly shook his head. "No, Jerry," he said thoughtfully, "the timing's bad. Everyone would tie it in with the things that the kids turned up this afternoon, and there'd be *more* trouble."

"But why couldn't you hold a confidential meeting? Why not pass it through and then keep it quiet until the end of school?"

"Nope," Condon demurred. "Rockwell's popular and the team's going good. Why, if the kids won the state championship again this year, Rockwell would be the toast of the town. Might even beat me out for mayor."

"But what if they lose," Davis persisted. "It's a vet-eran team and the fans in this town are hard losers. They'd blame Rockwell, wouldn't they? Wouldn't that be enough of an excuse along with his age and every-thing?"

Condon deliberated. "Probably would," he said slowly, "but what makes you think they'll lose?"

"Well, for one thing, Salem's the best team in the state and they'll probably win tomorrow and that'll knock the kids out of the race—unless Steeltown loses, too. Even if they do beat Salem and go to the state tournament, they haven't got a chance to win the championship. Nick Trullo's out with a bad arm and Hilton's the only other pitcher—"

"Hilton's good!"

"Sure he's good! But Rockwell wouldn't use a sling-shot unless it had three days' rest! And to win the cham-pionship you have to play three games in four days. Who's going to pitch? Besides," Davis said meaningly, "I happen to know a couple of guys who are out to get Hilton, but good. He'll be lucky if he gets to pitch *one* game!"

Condon's sharp eyes probed Jerry Davis' pale blue eyes deeply. Then he nodded decisively. "All right," he said shortly, "I'll do it! But your father will have to submit the proposal and force it through. Okay?"

Davis laughed confidently. "Don't worry about that! The old man hates Rockwell nearly as much as I do, and he's got Cantwell and Greer under his thumb. It's a cinch!"

John Schroeder and Doc Jones had dinner together that night at the Valley Hotel and spent nearly two hours laughing and talking about the day's events. The humorous aspects of the day's incidents were enjoyed by hundreds of other citizens that evening, too, but there were many who failed to find any humor whatever in the developments. Buck Adams and Peck Weaver were fighting mad and blaming their particular predicament on Henry Rockwell and Chip Hilton.

"That kid thinks he pulled a fast one, doesn't he?" Weaver growled.

"Yeah," Adams muttered, "that's what *he* thinks. He'll pay for this! Pay plenty!"

And Mike Sorelli was fuming and burning with anger as his eyes flashed back through the long narrow room and noted the inactivity. Normally, every table in the place would have been busy by this time. Mike decided to see Mayor Condon the first thing in the morning. He had spent a lot of time and money campaigning for that guy. A fellow couldn't make money running a poolroom unless he had players. And Mike Sorelli couldn't compete with the free pool in J. P. Ohlsen's recreation center unless he had certain inducements to offer.

Chip wanted to sleep well that night; get a complete rest so he would be in good shape for the game. But the strange bed and the long trip and thoughts of all the

things that had happened that day combined to cause
him a restless night. He was still tired when the Big
Reds took hitting practice the next afternoon. A little
later, warming up with Soapy, he saw Kip Parcels
throwing in front of the home dugout. It was to be
another duel of right-handers. He shifted his eyes
quickly to Nick Trullo lobbing the ball to Carl Carey.
Nick's arm was a little better, but not good enough
. . . He'd have to go all the way. . . .

A tremendous cheer greeted Kip Parcels when he
walked out to the mound to start the game. Parcels had
lost but one game all year, a 1–0 shutout to Chip Hilton and the Big Reds, and the home fans wanted to
even that score. So did Kip Parcels. Chip knew this was
going to be another last-out battle after Parcels' first
pitch. Kip had all his stuff, and he retired the Big Reds
in order.

Chip's fatigue vanished as soon as he toed the rubber; he was fast and his control was perfect. He matched
Parcels' performance, but it required more throws. The
Sailors were waiting him out, looking over every pitch,
working him to the limit. It was good strategy. This
was the fifth straight game he had worked, five games
in fifteen days.

Going into the last of the seventh, Parcels had nine
strike-outs and had held the Big Reds to two singles.
Chip had set eleven Sailors down on strikes and had yet
to yield a hit. But the home-crowd stretch was a bad
omen. The first hitter topped a slow roller toward
Badger and streaked for first. The "arm" swooped in on
the ball and fielded it perfectly with a bare-hand
pickup. Then Chuck fired the ball in a continuous un-
derhand throw to first. The stocky infielder had made
this throw all year and not once had it gotten away.
But this time the ball took off in a fast rising slant over

Biggie Cohen's head, and out to Carl Carey in the right-field corner. The runner lit out for second, made the turn, and gambled on Carl's arm. It was a good gamble, and he went into third standing up. Carey's throw was wide of the base.

The home fans were up on their feet when the ball sailed over Biggie's head and they remained up. This was the break of the game. All at once Chip felt tired, had that let down feeling which grips a fellow in a tense moment of emotional stress. Then he gave his first walk of the game and that put runners on first and third, none away.

The runner on first scampered down to second on the very next pitch. Soapy didn't even try the throw. Then the Salem fans really had themselves a time, for one of Chip's screwballs got clear away from Soapy and before he could retrieve the bounding sphere, both runners had scored. Chip came to life then, striking that hitter out and getting the next two on pop-ups to Cohen and Badger.

Those two runs gave Parcels something to work on and he followed through beautifully. He had the Big Reds eating out of his hand. Chip followed suit and when the visitors trotted in for the top of the ninth, it was "now or never."

Right then and there they got a shot in the arm. Several unimportant scores came over the public address system, but the last one was the thriller.

"Southern 9, Steeltown 7!"

The Big Reds' cheer was spontaneous, but it died just as fast. Steeltown's loss meant a sure tie for the runner-up spot . . . But if they could win . . . if they could take the Sailors . . . they'd be in the play-offs!

Soapy was up, freckled face sober and determined. And the old school try paid off! Soapy slashed a grasscutter through the box and over the keystone sack for the Big Reds' third hit of the game. Chip, in the circle, turned toward the dugout for instructions, but Rockwell waved him toward the plate, signaling that he was on his own.

Parcels hadn't forgotten that other game and the screaming liner his opponent had smashed into right center. Kip remembered too well how Chip Hilton had stretched the hit into a three-bagger that led to the only and winning run of the game. He looked toward the dugout and called time.

Chip knew what the Sailors had decided in the brief huddle as soon as Parcels began throwing for the corners. Kip wasn't going to give him anything good, but neither was he going to put the tying run on first. So Chip waited them out, waited for the good one that never came. But, as he trotted down to first, he was just as happy. The tying run was on now, and there was no one down. He swiftly calculated Cohen's position in the batting order. Tuffy, Speed, Red, and then Biggie . . . If they could only get another runner on, Biggie would do it. Biggie had to do it! . . .

Rockwell's hand showed then. He knew this was the big break and that a mistake now would probably mean the loss of the game. The Big Reds hadn't been able to hit the size of their hats against Parcels in two games, and that decided him. He'd lay it down and keep laying it down until he could get Cohen up there to win the game.

Tuffy Collins was the Big Reds' lead-off hitter and he could bunt with the best of them. Tuffy delivered, as per orders, dropping a shallow one fifteen feet down the third-base line, the ball hopping back almost as soon as it lit. The Sailor third sacker, playing up, got the ball all right, pivoted for the throw to third, then changed his mind, and threw to first. But Tuffy's short legs could move and he beat the throw by a step. Chip, dancing off second, breathed a deep sigh of relief. Biggie would get his lick, now, if someone on base didn't get caught.

Speed Morris had hit in the Big Reds "push along" slot for three years, could place a bunt on a dime, and run like a deer. Rockwell unhesitatingly made the decision and the sign for the bunt came through. Speed justified Rockwell's confidence, squeezing Soapy home, advancing Chip to third and Tuffy to second. And he nearly beat Parcels' throw to first. That brought in the first run of the game for the Big Reds with one away and Schwartz at bat. Red was a steady slugger, and hit in the number three spot. He was good in the clutch.

Rockwell knew the Big Reds and he was sticking to his guns. Again the sign for the squeeze came through, and again the play worked. Chip was in like a streak of lightning, flashing across the plate with the tying run before a disgusted Kip Parcels could make the play at home. But his string-throw to first had Red by twenty feet. So there they were, all tied up, with Tuffy and the winning run on third, two away, and Biggie Cohen at bat.

So far, the big southpaw had been able to reach Parcels safely but once in seven trips to the plate. But thirty seconds later he had raised the average to .250, Tuffy Collins had scored to put the Big Reds ahead 3 to 2, and Biggie was standing on second base. But that was the end of the "big break." Chuck Badger went down swinging and Biggie died on the keystone bag.

Chip's tired feeling disappeared when Tuffy stomped across the plate with the run which broke the tie. In fact, Chip felt as though he hadn't thrown a ball in a month when he dusted his fingers with the resin bag after his warm-up. Then he turned on the heat and hopped his fast one past the hitters, setting the Sailors down in one-two-three order, and putting the Big Reds in the state championship play-offs.

Main Street was dark and deserted when the bus pulled into Valley Falls that night. Two or three dim lights gave evidence that a few all-night restaurants were still open and irrepressible Soapy organized a hamburger party. But Chip hurried home, anxious to tell his mother about the game.

Mary Hilton was awake and slipped quietly down to greet her son. She kissed Chip tenderly and then listened to his description of the game. When Chip finished, she thrust the papers into his hands.

"Read the stories, Chip," she said excitedly, "they're sensational. All I've heard since yesterday afternoon has been about the seniors and your 'administration.' Every person in town is talking about it."

Chip eagerly scanned the paper his mother had just given him.

CITY ADMINISTRATORS' FACES RED

High School Seniors Responsible

Friday, June 18, will long be remembered in Valley Falls. The officials of this city experienced an uneasy time of it yesterday because of Senior Day and the developments promise to last for many days to come. The student administration was directed by a teen-age mayor, William "Chip" Hilton, and the ground which was covered in his brief tenure speaks volumes for his organizing ability.

The "mayor" was the first to take over and worked all morning at his desk. After a short speech at the Chamber of Commerce luncheon, Mayor Hilton called a meeting of the City Council and several important matters were brought to that body's attention. First, it was resolved that the school board be reshuffled. Second, that all city administrators be enjoined from personally interfering with the conduct of school management.

Third, a surprise enforcement of many of the forgotten city ordinances was recommended and a list was turned over to Sheriff Nicholas Trullo and a special staff of deputies for enforcement. The final matter of importance and the move which was responsible for most of the administration's embarrassment was the decision to swear in one hundred special police, boys and girls, to process and serve under the direction of Police Chief, Bernie Cohen, and the Chief of Detectives, Robert Smith, a multitude of warrants, injunctions, and subpoenas.

Space does not permit a complete reporting of all of the actions placed on the books, but the following selection attests to the comprehension of the coverage:

1. A raid on a South Side gambling establishment, operated by two well-known hoodlums, was successful. Accompanying reporters and photographers substantiated the evidence. Cards, gambling slips, and other gaming material were confiscated.
2. Three adult poker games were broken up. One of these, a lunch hour penny-ante game, has been operating for many years in the second-floor office of one of Valley Falls' most popular physicians.
3. The proprietor of a local poolroom was served with a subpoena for permitting gambling in the form of Kelly pool in his "emporium."
4. Fire escapes on several buildings were condemned and a number of building operators were advised that their fire escapes were inadequate.
5. The one-day Fire Chief, George Browning, and other city officers, tried to condemn the city high school as a firetrap, but were overruled by the council.

Valley Falls' citizens got a laugh out of the highhanded action of the teen-age "city fathers," but there are many thoughtful grownups who see more than the antics of youthful jokers in the lively one-day administration. This paper suspects that the boys and girls were giving their elders a lesson in civics. And it is also suspected that some timely and sensible reforms may come about because of the "one-day" government.

Chip was relieved. "It isn't as bad as I had expected, Mother," he said earnestly. "Gee, I've been worried to death."

Mary Hilton patted her tall son on the shoulder and smiled brightly. "*Never* worry about doing the *right* thing, Chip," she said softly. "Now, let's go to bed."

The excitement and events of the past two days had exacted a heavy toll from Chip's reserve strength, and now that his mind was at ease, he fell asleep almost as soon as his head touched the pillow. And in the next room, Mary Hilton, happy to have her son home, safe in bed, breathed a little prayer of thankfulness. She was especially glad that Chip had not seen the accusing article which Muddy Waters had splashed on the front page of the *Times* and which bitterly attacked the ill-advised tomfoolery of certain members of Henry Rockwell's baseball team.

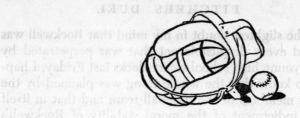

CHAPTER 13

BLUEPRINT FOR REVENGE

EARLY Monday morning five prominent Valley Falls citizens were sitting in the council room waiting for Mayor Condon. Two of the men, Jim Stanton and George Thomas, were uneasy and wary. The events of the past few days had cut them to the quick. They weren't sure they wanted to continue actively in the present city administration. The fact that J. P. Ohlsen was out of town and that the special meeting had been called in spite of his absence also gave them deep concern.

On the opposite side of the table, lined up side by side as usual, Jerry Davis, Sr., Frank Greer, and Fred Cantwell were talking in low voices. These three men worked hand in glove with Condon and cared not at all who knew it. When the mayor entered a few minutes later, their amiable welcome contrasted sharply with the reserved greeting of Stanton and Thomas.

Condon was in a bad mood and made no attempt to temper the viciousness of his immediate attack upon Rockwell.

"This man has gone too far," he said angrily. "There

115

isn't the slightest doubt in my mind that Rockwell was behind every despicable act that was perpetrated by those young high school smart alecks last Friday. I happen to know that the whole thing was planned by the senior members of the baseball team and that in itself is an indictment of the moral stability of Rockwell's leadership.

"I have called this special meeting to determine just what action we should take to remedy the situation— Yes, Jerry?"

Jerry Davis, Sr., proprietor of the largest jewelry store in the valley, was completely wrapped up in his oldest son. He had come well prepared for the opening he saw now and quickly followed Condon's lead.

"You're right, Mayor," he said firmly. "I, too, feel the time has come when we should do something about Rockwell's retirement. The man has outlasted his usefulness and, if this meeting is in order, I should like to move that Henry Rockwell be retired with full pension consideration and benefits at the end of the current school year."

The grim lines around Condon's mouth relaxed while Davis was speaking and he was nodding in agreement at the end. "The meeting is in order and the motion is—"

"But what about J. P.?" Stanton interrupted. "It seems to me this is something which could wait a few days."

"You forget this is the last week of school," Condon said evenly. "In view of that fact, and since we have a quorum, I believe we should proceed. Your motion is acceptable, Jerry, and we'll consider it the first order of business. Any discussion?"

There was a lot of discussion. And opposition. Stanton and Thomas battled so vigorously and so long that Condon finally agreed to pigeonhole formal action if Rockwell's Big Reds won the state championship. But he insisted on the vote and, as expected, the motion was carried.

After the vote and decision had been recorded, Condon suggested the action be kept strictly confidential.

"We'll see how the team comes out in the championship games," he said agreeably. "If they win, we'll forget about it until later in the summer."

Valley Falls High School teachers had their hands full that day. The "day" and the play-off championships took precedence over books and recitations and there was so much enthusiasm that most of the instructors gave up and joined in the unofficial celebration.

Chip hurried down to the Sugar Bowl that evening, stopping long enough at the soda fountain to look over Petey's shoulder at the sports page of the *Post* and note the pairing for the championship play-off games:

STATE BASEBALL PLAY-OFFS

VALLEY FALLS MEETS SEABURG

Wednesday Morning

The Big Reds will travel by bus to University Tuesday afternoon to defend their state baseball championship. The champs will face Seaburg, winner of Section Four laurels, in their first game, Wednesday morning. The locals are favored to win the opener chiefly because Coach Henry Rockwell has announced William "Chip" Hilton will start on the mound. What Rockwell will do for a pitcher in the Friday game—if the opener is won—presents a real problem because Nick Trullo is still nursing a sore arm. When questioned concerning his pitching plans after Wednesday, the veteran coach quipped: "We're playing them one at a time!"

Hilton is a strong thrower, in good form, and could undoubtedly pitch Wednesday and Friday. That would give Trullo three additional days to rest his sore arm and get ready for the final game, but Rockwell has never been

known to deviate from his rule that a high school pitcher be
given three days of rest. And he will probably start Smith
in the second game and hope for the best.

Should Valley Falls get by Seaburg Wednesday morning,
the Big Reds will play the winner of the Edgemont-Clinton
game Friday afternoon. The complete draw follows:

Thursday morning	* Salem II Rutledge IV	_____
		Friday morning _____
Wednesday afternoon	* Coreyville I Bloomfield III	_____
		Saturday afternoon _____
Thursday afternoon	* Edgemont III Clinton I	_____
		Friday afternoon _____
Wednesday morning	* Seaburg IV Valley Falls II	_____

* Sectional Champions

"Some draw," Petey said, "the Seabees are tough!"

Chip smiled wryly. "They're all tough in a tournament, Petey," he said gravely.

"Who's gonna pitch Friday?"

"You read what Rock said—"

"That's no answer, Chip," Petey pleaded. "No fooling,
what *are* you guys gonna do for a chucker on Friday?"

"What makes you think we'll be playing Friday?"

"Because you're pitching Wednesday!" Petey said
stoutly.

Chip laughed. "Wish I had your confidence. Maybe
Nick will be all right by Friday, Petey," he said hopefully. "He'd better be, or else—"

"Or else what?"

"Or else Soapy Smith!"

"Oh, *no!*"

"Oh, *yes!*"

Despite Petey's pleas for more information, Chip hurried back to the storeroom. There, John Schroeder, shuffling some papers at the desk, was absorbed in his work and Chip slipped quietly down the steps leading to the cellar. He had a lot of unpacking ahead of him if the Sugar Bowl was to operate efficiently during the four days he would be up at State. That thought brought a wry smile to his lips. He'd be back in Valley Falls Wednesday night . . . if he wasn't right Wednesday morning. . . .

Doc Jones was everyone's friend. Maybe that was why he knew everything that happened in Valley Falls just about as soon as it occurred. Undoubtedly, his close friendship with certain members of the City Council was responsible for the "confidential" information that he blurted out to Schroeder in the storeroom a few minutes after Chip had started his work in the cellar. When he heard Jones's ponderous tread and rasping voice, Chip smiled.

"John, what do you think I just learned?"

Chip had no desire to eavesdrop, but there wasn't much he could do about it—every word penetrated through to the cellar clear as a bell. He heard the creak of the chair as Schroeder swung about, and as Jones continued, Chip's smile vanished and his face sobered.

"The council voted for Rockwell's retirement at the end of the term? What do you think of that?"

"Oh, now, Doc, that can't be right! Someone's stringing you along."

"No, John, I got it straight from Stanton. Condon forced it through at a special meeting today. Vote was three to two— Ohlsen wasn't there!"

"You sure Stanton wasn't pulling your leg, Doc? Why, it's impossible—"

"It's not impossible and Stanton wasn't kidding. He was dead serious and pretty sick about it. In fact, he and George are planning to resign. They're just waiting for Ohlsen to get back."

"Can't believe it! No one's worried about Rock's age! Why, he's as fit as a fiddle!"

"He's that, all right. Must be young Davis and Cantwell and that crowd. They've been after Rockwell for a long time. Never thought they'd ever get any support, though.

"Oh, yes, Jim told me they did get Condon to say he'd hold everything off if the baseball team won the state tournament."

"He'd better," Schroeder said grimly. "If Rockwell brings back the championship after all the trouble he's had this year, this town will *give* him the high school. Personally, I think Condon's looking for trouble. People are getting fed up with him and his crowd. About time, too!"

Jones grunted. "You can say that again," he said grimly. "The kids opened the eyes of more than one person in this village. You going to the meeting? Well, come on then. We're late."

Long after Schroeder and Jones had departed, Chip sat on the box he had been unpacking, elbows on knees and chin in hands. Looking at the boy sitting there so quietly, you would have thought he was day-dreaming, resting from his work, half asleep. But Chip's mind was filled with a thousand bitter thoughts, all confused and all revolving around the shocking news he had just overheard. Long minutes later when he had gotten to his feet and had resumed his work, he was still thoughtful, but no longer confused. Now Chip Hilton and the

Big Reds had something else to fight for in their championship quest up at State.

Valley Falls gave the Big Reds a real send-off, lining the sidewalks from one end of Main Street to the other to cheer the red-and-white bus on its way. The school band, one hundred strong, led the way. Petey hadn't forgotten his usual treat and came tearing out of the Sugar Bowl with a big box of sandwiches and ice cream pops.

"Bring it back, gang," he shouted. "We'll be waiting up Saturday night!"

Then they were on their way, singing and cheering, and Valley Falls and all the troubled, doubtful days through which the team had passed, fighting to stay in the Sectional, were forgotten. Forgotten to all of the boys in that happy crowd except Chip Hilton. Chip was listening and laughing with the rest, but his mind was busy with thoughts of Rockwell. He nudged his seatmate.

"How's your arm, Nick?"

The big southpaw pursed his lips tight together and shook his head doubtfully. "It doesn't feel too good, Chip," he said in a low voice, "but it'll be all right when I need it. It's got to be all right! I've *got* to win one of those games. You can win the other two. Don't worry, I'll be all right!"

Buck Adams and Peck Weaver were in the crowd of Valley Falls baseball fans who lined Main Street. After the bus passed from sight, they walked gloomily down the street, headed for Mike Sorelli's poolroom.

"We didn't do so good," Peck said sourly. "We better give up!"

Adams grunted angrily. "I never give up! I started out to get those two birds and I'm gonna do it!"

"How?"

"Don't know yet."

"Well, you better hurry up. They're playin' Wednesday morning— Hey, there's Waters and Davis. Hiya, Jerry. Hiya, Muddy. How ya doin'?"

"Okay, I guess," Davis said shortly. "Looks like we rooted 'em in, all right."

"We're not through," Adams said aggressively. "Not yet!"

"Hope you're right," Davis said thoughtfully. "Confidentially, Rockwell's going to be tossed out on his ear if he doesn't bring the championship back."

Adams stopped in his tracks. "You mean that?" he asked, looking from Davis to Waters.

Davis' pale blue eyes were hard and cold and his voice grated angrily. "Sure do," he said harshly. "Well, see you up at the University."

"You won't see us," Adams growled, "but if what you said is straight, you can bet Rockwell won't be around here next year!"

Adams and Weaver spent the rest of that afternoon and most of the evening trying to evolve a plan. And, as usual, it was Buck who came up with the answer. It was beautiful in its simplicity.

"Look, Peck," he said triumphantly, "all we've got to do is get that fresh kid's moniker on a fake contract—"

"Oh, yeah," growled Weaver. "Would you mind tellin' me how we're goin' to—"

"Leave that to me. I got me an idea. And when we flash that contract around the night before Hilton's s'posed to pitch, the newshounds'll go to work, and Rockwell's fair-haired boy will be out of there. But good!"

"I don't get it," muttered Weaver doubtfully.

Adams' shrewd and fertile imagination was now hitting on all cylinders. Impatiently he explained: "Don't you get it, you dope? Why, it's easy as duck soup. All we gotta do is get someone to go up there to University and get Hilton's name on a fake contract, show it to a coupla sports writers, and we're in! And the pretty boy's out! Get it?"

"Yeah, I guess so," Weaver said uncertainly. "But who you gonna get to do the job? It's gotta be a stranger. Someone Hilton doesn't know and someone the sports writers don't know. Some guy they'll never see again."

"Right! And I know just the guy! Dutch Swarts!"

Weaver nodded doubtfully. "Yeah," he agreed reluctantly, "Dutch might be okay if you can keep him sober— If you don't pay him off till the job's finished."

The State Athletic Association was a powerful organization, backed up by the administrators of every high school in the state, as well as by the state legislature. And it was a generous and hospitable organization. When it sponsored a game, a tournament, or a play-off series, the members of the arrangement and entertainment committees were instructed to be lavish where the participating teams were concerned.

Those in charge had really "gone to town" this year. The State, largest hotel in the city of University, had agreed to house all eight teams. And when the Big Reds arrived, the lobby, the adjoining restaurant, coffee shop, and the sidewalk outside were jammed with a milling crowd of happy ballplayers and rooters. Their arrival was greeted boisterously.

"Here comes the Valley boys!"

"Hey, there, Big Reds, hey!"

"Better turn around, better pivot and go home!"

"Yeah, you won't be here long!"

"No championship for you guys this year!"

"Where's the cup? You bring it back?"

It was all good-natured ribbing and the Big Reds liked it. A fellow couldn't be blamed for lifting his chin a little higher and squaring his shoulders when he was on a championship club. Except for the size of the squad, the Big Reds looked like champions. Each boy was neatly dressed, clean-faced, and well set up. After they had checked in and polished off a big steak dinner, they mingled in the crowd, greeting old friends and making new acquaintances. But each Big Red kept his eye on the big timepiece above the desk and at nine o'clock every member of the squad was in the living room of Rockwell's suite.

"Now, if we can get by tomorrow and Friday, we'll have Chip for the championship game. That is, if Nick can work Friday and get by—"

"He'll get by!" the boys chorused.

"I'll work," Nick growled. "I'd like to see someone stop me!"

"You'll work if your arm's okay, Nick," Rockwell said firmly. "Your arm's more important than ten championships—

"Now, we'll take a long hike and when we get back we'll hit the hay. All of us! By this time tomorrow night, we'll either be on our way home or figuring the Friday game. Let's go!"

CHAPTER 14

GRAND-SLAM HOMER

THE red-and-white bus turned left with the wave of the officer's arm and rolled up the smooth road which was lined on each side by the ivy-covered buildings. Chip scarcely noted the beautiful green-carpeted campus; his eyes were focused on the top of the tall grandstand which he could see above the concrete wall extending away from the field house. And his heart was thumping when he dropped out of the bus to the walk in front of the field gate. The usual pre-game empty feeling gripped him, numbing the arm and hand carrying his uniform roll and turning his legs to rubber.

Chip's memories of Seaburg High School came flooding into mind. The first game he had ever pitched as a starting chucker had been against the Seabees. And he had come out of that game with a no-hitter. Most of the fellows who had played with Seaburg last year were back, including Thornton, the Seabees' star chucker whom he had beaten that day. Chip had a hunch Thornton and he would meet head-on again today.

Chip's hunch was right, for when he trotted through the tunnel and out on the field, the first Seabee he saw was Thornton. And Thornton was warming up in front of the Seaburg dugout.

But when Chip toed the warm-up rubber and heard the scattered cheers and yells of the Valley Falls rooters, his mind and every muscle of his body were concerned with one thing and one thing only—the game.

Before he knew it, hitting and fielding practice was over and he was sitting in a corner of the dugout holding his warm-up jacket close around his arm. Out on the hill, Thornton was blazing them in and Chip knew he had a fight on his hands. Thornton looked to be in top form.

The Big Reds, batting first, didn't get far that inning nor in the six innings which followed. Thornton was fast and his control was perfect. Chip pitched his heart out, calling on his fast ball, his slider, and his change-up to hold the Seabees scoreless for the first seven innings. But he knew he was tiring and he needed a run or two for a cushion. So instead of continuing on into the dugout when he came in for the top of the eighth, he stopped just outside and waited for his teammates. And as he stood there, it seemed as if all the Big Red rooters got the same idea; this was it! The big end of the batting order was up and now was the time. They began beating the boards with rhythmic stomping of the feet and the roar of their voices flooded the field with the demand for the big rally.

Tuffy Collins led off, spreading his stubby legs in a wide stance, vigorously thumping his bat on the plate. Tuffy knew how to work a pitcher, crouching and bobbing and weaving like a boxer until the strike zone seemed no larger than the catcher's glove. Thornton didn't like it. He tried too hard to strike out the aggressive little holler guy, and lost the battle of wits by issuing his first pass of the game. So there was one on, none down, and Speed Morris up. Speed took a called strike, a ball, and then dumped a perfect bunt to the right of the plate. The catcher, Thornton, and the Seabee first sacker all converged on the ball, each holding back for the other to field the ball, with the result that there was no play at all and Tuffy and Speed were both safe.

Red Schwartz marched up to the plate then, swinging his bat, eager to bust one on the nose. But Rockwell had his two fastest runners at first and second and Red followed orders with a bunt smack in front of the plate. The Seabees' receiver pounced on the ball like a cat, but Tuffy and Speed had moved with Red's pivot, and Tuffy slid into third in a cloud of dust a good two seconds before the ball smacked into the third sacker's glove. And the bases were loaded with nobody down.

The Valley Falls rooters really let loose then, sending a roar of exultation across the field that drowned out the Seabee shouts as though they were whispers. Chip was on his feet yelling with the rest when Biggie Cohen stepped into the batter's box, and he was still yelling seconds later when the Big Reds' first sacker trotted across the plate following a grand-slam homer. Biggie had come through, and although there was no more scoring, the four-run cushion was enough. Chip breezed them by the Seaburg hitters one-two-three in the bottom of the eighth and the ninth and the Big Reds were in the semifinals.

That evening Chip called his mother and then joined Biggie and Soapy in the lobby. It was a strange scene that greeted him, strange for a big hotel. For the lobby and the shops surrounding it were mobbed with groups of youngsters with tanned faces, all talking and laughing and brimming over with baseball.

Competition for baseball talent is keen and this tournament had its full quota of scouts. At that very moment, the ivory hunters were seated at one long table in the main dining room, jabbering and wisecracking like tobacco auctioneers. But underneath the pleasantries and gibes there was plenty of serious thought. And, as the players who had performed that day were discussed, each scout cocked an ear for information which might help him confirm his own opinions.

"Whaddaya think of that Hilton kid?"

"Cute! Got a lot on the ball!"

"Lotsa kids throw hard," someone drawled. "I didn't see no change-up."

"Change-up?" another snorted. "What's he need a change-up for? He's fast and he's got control! I could teach him a change-up throw in a week! The kid's good!"

"Maybe he didn't show his change-up," someone suggested.

"Me, I like that other kid," another voice broke in. "Thornton, or something like that—"

"I go along with *that* boy. He mixes up his pitches like a kid with a set of blocks."

"Aw, he's curve-happy. You saw what that big lefty did to one of his hooks."

And that's the way it went, each scout expressing his views, sometimes exaggerated and sometimes understated.

Later they converged on the lobby, mingling with the kids, moving close to the players in which they were interested.

This maneuvering was nothing new. Some of the players had been approached several times during the season and most of the scouts were well known. Chip knew Stu Gardner, of course, but practically all of the others were strangers to him. Not that he didn't know them by reputation. Some were national figures and had been featured in magazines and papers all over the country.

Rumors had been flying all day about the boys in whom the scouts were most interested and Chip was glad his name was prominent on the list. Not that it meant he was interested in an immediate big-league career; college was his first objective. But it made him feel good just the same.

Stu Gardner sighted Chip, Biggie, and Soapy and joined their little circle. Gardner was smiling. "Nice going, kids," he said happily. "You look like the class of the tournament to me!"

Soapy winked and nodded his head. "You tell 'em!" he said, smiling broadly. "We'll kill 'em! You see Biggie lay into that one in the top of the eighth? And how about the way Chipper, here, mowed 'em down? I tell you, we'll kill 'em!"

That brought a laugh from everyone within hearing distance. In two short days Soapy's *"We'll kill 'em!"* had become as well known as his flaming red hair in the coaching box and behind the plate. The burst of laughter drew attention to them and several other scouts elbowed their way in their direction. The circle grew until it filled the center of the lobby, the boys intent and asking the questions while the scouts obligingly answered with "behind the scenes" stories of the big leagues.

Chip was gradually crowded to the outside fringe of the circle. Then, finding it difficult to hear, he moved over to a big plate-glass window by the street and sat down in one of the leather-covered settees. He was soon engaged in the fascinating pastime of watching the passers-by and speculating about their personalities. So absorbed was he, in fact, that he was startled by a man's voice saying:

"What are you doing over here all by yourself?"

Chip turned and glanced up quickly. The speaker was a tall, friendly-faced man, whom Chip recognized as Perry Crane, a scout for the Eagles. Without waiting for a reply, Crane sat down on the settee and stretched his long legs out comfortably. Then he extended a broad, sun-tanned hand.

"My name's Crane, Hilton. I'm a member of the scouting fraternity, as you can probably guess. Saw you work today. Nice throwing!"

Chip smiled as he shook Crane's hand. "Thank you, Mr. Crane," he said hesitantly. "I had more than my share of luck, I guess."

"Been lucky a lot of times in the last couple of years, it seems to me," Crane drawled, "judging from your record. Today was the first time I ever saw you work. Not that I haven't heard about you," he continued hurriedly. "By the way, what are you planning to do after graduation?"

Chip had heard of Perry Crane. The man was known as a big-time operator, just like Stu Gardner. He had the reputation of being one of the best big-league scouts in the business. Crane was, Chip judged, in his fifties, well set up, clean-shaven, with steady brown eyes and a pleasant smile.

"I hope to go to college, Mr. Crane," Chip said slowly, watching the scout's face anxiously. "That is," he continued, "if everything works out all right."

Crane smiled warmly. "Everything will work out all right," he said, nodding his head and tapping Chip on the chest. "Everything will work out just the way you want it—if you want it badly enough! That's one of the wonderful things about this great country of ours—a fellow can do almost anything he sets out to do, providing it's honest, and he is honest in his desires and is willing to pay the price in study and work. Why—"

For the next hour Crane talked to Chip about the youngsters he had met, about those who had jumped at the opportunity to play professional baseball and about those who had preferred another profession. He lauded Henry Rockwell for the coach's contention that a boy who was qualified to do college work and who could profit by the opportunity should continue his schooling.

"More and more every year," he said, "college players are going into the big leagues. College kids get good coaching and they're still youngsters when they finish their studies. Then, if something goes wrong in their professional ball careers, they've got a good background for something else."

Crane then described the opportunities in big-league baseball, the pitfalls, and the rewards. But not once did he attempt to discourage Chip's college ambitions.

Long after Crane had departed, Chip sat there thinking about baseball and the men who were responsible for making it such a great game. And he was proud that he had met Stu Gardner and Perry Crane and that he had been coached by a man like the Rock. Now, just when his high school career was ending, he could understand many of the things that had puzzled him during the four short years he had played for Valley Falls High School. The Rock's battle for discipline and training and the importance of a fellow keeping up with his studies . . . Lots of the fellows had thought Rockwell's constant reiteration of the importance of schoolwork was because he and the team might be deprived of a player's participation through scholastic difficulties. Chip had known better then and he knew better now; he knew that the interests of a real coach, a coach like the Rock, extended far beyond a game, a season, and even a championship.

Thoughts of Rockwell brought him back to his surroundings with a start. The coach had called skull practice for nine o'clock. Chip glanced at his watch and then dashed for the elevator. He was ten minutes late!

It was so quiet when Chip paused outside Parlor A that he was sure he must be mistaken in the room number. But when he cautiously turned the knob and opened the door it was to meet a warning battery of eyes from his teammates and a cold glare from Henry Rockwell. But that was all. Rockwell continued his rundown of Clinton's batting order and then discussed every bit of possible baseball strategy that might enable the Big Reds to get by the semifinals and into the championship game. At ten o'clock, Valley Falls' Big Reds baseball champions lit out for a fifteen-minute hike and then went to bed full of baseball, confidence, and determination.

Baseball was the chief topic that evening in Valley Falls, too. The story of the game had reached the ears of most Big Reds home rooters by way of the radio and Stan Gomez. Buck Adams and Peck Weaver were among those who had heard the broadcast, and for the first time that year they were in a happy mood.

"We're in," Adams said jubilantly. "Now all we want is for Trullo to win Friday afternoon."

"But what if Trullo loses?" Weaver objected.

"So what? That'll put Valley Falls out and Rockwell out, and that's what we want, isn't it?"

"Yeah, but how about our bets?"

"Heck with the bets. We're out to get even with Rockwell and Hilton. Anyway, we won't bet until the championship game. Everything's perfect! We'll pick up Swarts Friday morning and drive him up to University and have him do his stuff Friday night. And Saturday morning Rockwell will think an atom bomb had lit on his baseball team!"

CHAPTER 15

COSTLY AUTOGRAPH

CHIP was grinning happily when he finished the letter to his mother. Then he reread for the tenth time the newspaper clipping he was sending home. The past two days had been exciting and eventful and he was reluctant to lose any part of the memory of all that had occurred.

SALEM MEETS VALLEY FALLS FOR CHAMPIONSHIP

Section Two Contenders Meet in Title Game Tomorrow

Underdog Valley Falls High School ball club, handicapped all season by injuries and a two-man pitching staff, fought an uphill battle yesterday afternoon to win out over Clinton High School by a score of 9 to 8. Nick Trullo, the Big Reds' ailing number two chucker, was hit freely, but the support of his teammates was sensational. Time and again clutch plays saved the day. It was the ninth inning two-base pinch hit by Hilton which sent Cohen, the Valley Falls cleanup hitter, in with the winning run. With two down in the bottom of the ninth, Clinton ahead 8 to 7, and Schwartz and Cohen on first and second respectively, Coach Henry Rockwell sent Hilton in to hit for Badger. The tall, rangy chucker pulled a screaming liner across the first-base bag and clear to the fence scoring Schwartz and Cohen and breaking up the game.

So, for the first time, two baseball teams from the same section have won through to the finals. Salem, as expected, outhit and outscored Bloomfield in the morning semifinal, 8 to 2.

Salem won the Section Two championship by winning 14 of a 16-game schedule, while Valley Falls barely got under the wire ahead of Steeltown to win the runner-up spot with an 11–4 record. The ace hurlers of each club, Salem's Kip Parcels and Valley Falls' Chip Hilton, are slated to start. Hilton bested Parcels twice during the regular season to give Salem their only setbacks and that fact has established the Valley champions as the favorites in the opinion of most experts. The duel between these two youngsters will highlight the most successful championship series in the forty-year history of the State High School Athletic Association.

In addition to the five thousand fans who will be on hand at two o'clock game time, every big-league chain will be represented by one or more scouts. Talent galore will be on display. Heading the stars are two of the state's leading hurlers, Hilton and Parcels. Outstanding infielders from both teams include Salem's hot corner flash, George Curry; Valley Falls' speedy shortstop, Speed Morris; and the Big Reds' hard-hitting first sacker, Biggie Cohen. Salem undoubtedly has the greatest outfield ever to play in a state series. Phil Hartman, Brady O'Shea, and Bill Erickson are fast, good throwers, and long-ball hitters. The edge in the receiving department goes to the Sailors because no boy in the state can match the know-how and throwing ability of Butch "The Arm" Overton.

Chip folded the clipping carefully, stamped the envelope with special delivery stamps, and started for the lobby. His mother would receive the letter tomorrow morning at the telephone office if he could get to 'the post office before seven o'clock. He glanced at his watch. It was six forty-five and he had plenty of time. But he had forgotten about the jammed lobby. It had never been so crowded as this and, as he elbowed his way through the throng, he was greeted from all sides.

"Hiya, Hilton! How's the flipper?"

"Hey, Chip! Wait a minute!"

"What's the rush? Where you goin'?"

Chip tried to explain that he was in a hurry to get to the post office but that made no impression on the boisterous youngsters. They kidded him unmercifully.

"Post office? Better take a bodyguard!"

"Yeah, Salem's gonna kidnap *you!*"

"Got any insurance on that wing?"

"How's about an autograph?"

"Yeah, sign mine, too! I'm from Salem!"

It was good-natured joshing and Chip took it in stride as he slowly made his way toward the street. Then the crowd parted and Biggie came rolling through like a giant bulldozer. Soapy and Red followed in his wake and Chip fell in behind the trio and gained the sidewalk. But he wasn't through yet. Someone grabbed him by the arm.

"Excuse me. Ain't you Chip Hilton?"

Chip turned to face a middle-aged stranger. The man was carelessly dressed and his face was flushed as he fumbled in his pocket.

"I—er—my kid's one of your fans and I promised him I'd get your autograph. He's sick and— Wait till I get my pen.

"Here, just sign on the bottom of this paper. Wish it was a baseball contract. Looks like one at that! Haven't signed a contract yet, have you? Well, we'll just consider this is one. Some joke, eh? That's right! Right there! That's swell! Thanks a million! Good luck to-morrow!"

The man was gone before Chip realized that he was still holding the pen. He started after the stranger, but he had disappeared in the crowd.

"*He* was in a hurry," Biggie drawled. "No one ever gets that excited over *my* autograph!"

"That's *nothing*," Soapy said ruefully. "No one even *asks* me for my autograph!"

"I'm sorry about the pen," Chip said worriedly, "he probably needs it. Maybe he'll come back. Gee, I'd wait, but I want to get this letter in the mail."

"Here," Schwartz said quickly, "give it to me. I'll wait and you can pick me up on your way back."

Fifteen minutes later they found Schwartz in the same spot and he still had the pen.

"Don't worry about it," Soapy said, "he knows where you are. He'll show up."

A few blocks away, Adams and Weaver waited impatiently in a parked car for their envoy to return. Dutch Swarts was about as dependable as April weather and the two plotters were well aware of that fact.

"You give him any money?" Weaver demanded.

Adams laughed shortly. "Think I'm nuts," he said irritably. "He gets his dough when the job's finished. Gettin' the autograph's the easiest part of the deal. Big thing's to fool the writers. Make them think he's legit."

"Yeah," Weaver agreed. "He'll hafta be good. Those writers ain't dumbbells. Think he can do it?"

"Wouldn't be here if I didn't," Adams said worriedly. "He's smart enough, all right, but I'm not too sure he looks the part. Most of those big-league scouts are nifty dressers. Another thing, most writers know the big-league scouts."

"The jokers coverin' these games don't know them,"

Weaver said. "Anyway, have him play up to one of the local—" He nudged Adams excitedly. "Here he comes now!"

Swarts quickened his pace as he approached the car, then opened the back door and dropped down on the seat.

"Get it?" Adams demanded.

"Sure," Swarts said casually, pulling the paper from his pocket. "It was a cinch!"

Adams unfolded the paper and held it close to the light of the dashboard. It was an impressive looking document even in that dim light. At the top of the first page "Contract" was printed in large letters. "The Chicago Bisons Baseball Club" completed the heading. On the signature line, written in ink, was the name "Chip Hilton."

Buck turned and slapped Swarts on the knee. "So far so good," he said approvingly. "I'll just sign for Mary Hilton and then we'll get goin'. Now comes the tough part. First, we're gonna dress you up in one of my suits and go through a little rehearsal. That's why we checked in at the motel outside of town. Get goin', Peck!"

Dutch Swarts wasn't a bad-looking fellow. Nor, indeed, was he bad at heart. He was one of those unfortunate men who are morally weak, unable to resist certain temptations. Swarts's weakness was drink. He was a confirmed alcoholic and his only ambition was to earn enough money to satisfy that relentless craving.

An hour later Adams and Weaver surveyed him critically and then grunted their approval.

Weaver chuckled. "You look sharp, kid," he said admiringly, "*real* sharp."

"He's gotta do more than *look* sharp," Adams warned. "Now listen—"

The next hour was spent in rehearsing every move Swarts was to make, and it was ten o'clock before Adams was satisfied. "Let's go," he said tersely, "we don't have much time."

It wasn't difficult to locate the baseball writers. Every night they joined the scouts and talked baseball. After the game it was dinner baseball, then lobby baseball, and finally tavern baseball. In between, like the scouts, they talked to the players and the coaches, getting leads for special articles and swapping stories with everyone they met.

It took Swarts nearly an hour to infiltrate the restless group and another half hour to maneuver close enough to one of the local writers to strike up a conversation. All the time, he kept shuffling several filing cards as though they were playing cards. Adams had written the name of the outstanding players on these cards and Swarts kept adding little notes on some, crossing out others, and occasionally balling one and tossing it over his shoulder. Curiosity finally got the better of Swarts's companion.

"That the way you keep track of your prospects?" he asked.

"Yeah, that's one way," Swarts replied.

"Who do you like?"

Swarts shuffled the cards quickly, noting the numbers Adams had placed in the corner of each card. "Well," he said cautiously, "I've got my eyes on several of 'em. Here's a pretty good boy—name's Thornton, a chucker—"

"That what you're interested in—pitchers?"

Swarts pursed his lips and eyed the questioner steadily. "Yeah," he drawled, "that's chiefly what I'm interested in—pitchers."

"Seems to me you've missed the best one."

Swarts shook his head. "Not me, mister!" he said shortly. "Look, I don't know what your game is, but mine's baseball. And particularly chuckers. I don't miss nobody!"

"What about that kid from Valley Falls? The Hilton kid?"

Swarts eyed his companion suspiciously. "What about him?" he asked.

"He's the best pitcher I ever saw for a kid, that's what about him!"

Swarts grinned. "Yeah, he ain't bad," he admitted cautiously, "not bad at all—"

Turk laughed derisively. This fellow must be cracked. Hilton was the best big-league prospect he had seen in years. He, himself, had been so impressed with the kid he'd asked the boy to sign his souvenir program. He elbowed Swarts. "Not bad," he repeated, "I'll say he isn't! Why, every scout and 'bird dog' in town is after *him!*"

Swarts laughed. "Won't do 'em no good," he said mysteriously, "they're wastin' their time! Listen, Bub—" Swarts paused, studied his acquaintance carefully for a long minute, and then continued abruptly. "I could let you in on a big secret if I was sure you wouldn't spill it."

Jimmy Turk was ambitious. He wanted to be a great sports writer and he was always on the alert for a scoop, a big story that he could break before anyone else. He had sensed that this mysterious baseball scout meant a story and he quickly reassured Swarts.

"Don't worry about that."

Swarts played his part perfectly. He glanced covertly around and then edged close to Turk. Cautiously pulling the contract out of his pocket, Swarts fumbled with the front page long enough for Turk to note that it was a baseball contract with the Bisons. Then he placed a finger under Chip's signature and tapped the "Mary Hilton" underneath.

"Lock, stock, and barrel," he gloated. "Is that a secret or is that a secret? Guess you understand now what I meant when I said a lot of guys were wastin' their time? 'Course we ain't gonna do no announcin' until the kid graduates, but he's signed tight enough. Get it?"

Turk got it all right, and his thoughts were racing. Here was the break he had been waiting for, the scoop of the tournament. He could scarcely restrain his jubilation, so anxious was he to get away and write the story. But he exercised a bit of caution. Fortunately, he reflected, he had gotten Chip Hilton's autograph just for fun, and he pictured the signature he had seen on the contract in his mind. He pulled the tournament program out of his pocket and carelessly turned the leaves until he came to the Valley Falls page.

His heart leaped. The signatures were identical. There was no doubt in Turk's mind now. This was the scoop to end all tournament scoops, and it was all his, provided he could get this fellow out of here before he told someone else about the contract. He shook his head admiringly. "Nice going! Why every scout in town's been after that kid. Say, let's get something to eat."

Swarts shook his head. "No, thanks," he said, affecting a yawn, "I'm dead tired. I think I'll turn in. So long, be sure to keep what I showed you under your hat until next week. The kid graduates Monday and it'll be in all the papers Tuesday. That's for sure!"

A few minutes later each was chuckling to himself as he hurried away. Turk wanted to get down to the office and get his story ready for the morning paper and Swarts wanted to report to Adams and get his money.

He had made up his mind to have a real weekend for himself. Adams thought differently.

"No dough," Buck growled. "No dough 'til we see tomorrow morning's paper."

"But, look, Buck," Swarts pleaded, "I did my part. What's the idea? You said I'd get paid as soon as I contacted the reporter—"

Adams shook his head. "Oh, no, Dutch," he said grimly, "I told you you'd get paid when the job was finished. That means when and if the story hits the paper."

"It'll hit the paper, all right! Aw, come on, Buck," Swarts pleaded, "let me have five bucks anyway."

"Nothin' doin'! You get paid in full tomorrow! We'll drop you off at the lodging house and you hit the hay and sleep late. We'll meet you at Tom and Jerry's at two o'clock tomorrow afternoon and you'll get paid in full— plus a bonus, if the story draws a headline. Now gimme that fake contract."

Swarts shook his head stubbornly. "Nothin' doin', Buck," he said sullenly, "you get the contract when I get paid. I'll be at Tom and Jerry's at two o'clock tomorrow."

After dropping Swarts at his lodging house, Adams headed the car back toward the center of town. As he drove through the deserted streets, he talked rapidly, half to himself and half to Weaver.

"Now, we've got to do our part. First, we gotta check that guy Turk and make sure he's writin' the story. He oughtta be at the newspaper office. Deadline for the paper is four in the morning— Then we gotta make a round of the right spots and place a few bets. And first thing in the morning we gotta place some more."

Weaver nodded understandingly. "Yeah, but what time does that paper come out?"

"Eleven o'clock! That's why we've got to be on the job first thing in the morning. Some of the books'll probably be suspicious as it is."

"Why don't we place all our money tonight?"

"Too late—and besides, something might go wrong. Most of the spots will be closed, anyway. Well, here we are. Now, we gotta see if that guy's writin' the story. You wait here in the car and I'll go up there and pretend to be lookin' for somethin' in one of last week's papers."

"Still think you oughtta call this Turk on the phone," Weaver said stubbornly.

Adams shook his head. "Nope," he said softly, "too risky. He might get suspicious."

"Don't see the difference," Weaver grumbled. "He's gonna get suspicious if you talk to him. Besides, if anything goes wrong later, he's liable to tie you into the deal."

"He won't see me," Adams said confidently. "You sit tight. I'll be right back."

And "right back" he was, jubilant and excited. "Okay, Buck," he said, scrambling into the car, "we're in! The guy's writin' the story right now! The elevator boy took me up and, on the way, I asked him if I could see one of last week's papers. He said 'there wasn't anyone up there but Turk' so I said forget it— Said I'd come back in the morning. Hah! Fat chance! I'll be busy in the morning, but it won't be readin' one of last week's papers!"

"Hilton and Rockwell're gonna be busy, too," Weaver gloated. "Busy tryin' to explain their way outta this one!"

"Might do it," Adams snickered, "but it'll be too late! Too late to win the game!"

CHAPTER 16

SCOOP STORY

STU GARDNER whistled under his breath and pressed the morning paper out flat on the counter, nearly upsetting the cup of coffee which he had been sipping.

"What's the matter, too hot?" the pleasant-faced waitress asked.

"I'll say!" Gardner replied. "Too hot to be true!" He swung around on the stool and startled the girl by bolting for the door. She looked after him with astonished eyes. Then she dipped a dainty finger in the cup of coffee. "That coffee isn't hot," she whispered in a shocked voice. "He must be crazy. And he seemed like such a nice man!"

Gardner's feet were racing almost as fast as his thoughts as he dashed through the door of the restaurant which led to the hotel lobby. "Can't be," he muttered, heading for the elevator, "just can't be! Something's wrong!"

143

At that precise moment Soapy was shaking the morning paper in Chip's face. "Look, Chip! Look at this!" he shouted, jabbing a finger into the paper. "What's this all about?"

Chip had been resting up for the game and he was half asleep when his startled eyes flashed from Soapy to the front-page headline. His first glance brought him upright and to his feet, wide awake.

VALLEY FALLS PITCHER FACES ELIGIBILITY CHARGE

COMMITTEE TO INVESTIGATE RUMOR OF BIG-LEAGUE CONTRACT

A Special Sports Story
By JIMMY TURK

William "Chip" Hilton, brilliant pitching star of the Valley Falls baseball team, is rumored to have signed a contract with the Chicago Bisons. Hilton was slated to pitch against Salem at two o'clock this afternoon in the final game of the state championship series.

Efforts to contact Hilton and Coach Henry Rockwell late last night were unsuccessful. Rockwell had left strict orders that neither he nor the Valley Falls players were to be disturbed.

A. K. Beldon, chairman of the State High School Athletic Association, was reached at his home in Steeltown and stated he had heard nothing of the rumor but that the matter would be discussed at the luncheon meeting of his committee today here in University.

If the rumor is substantiated, Hilton will not be permitted to pitch in today's game. The eligibility provisions of the High School Athletic Association specifically state that a high school athlete who signs a professional sports contract before the day following his graduation shall be immediately and automatically ineligible for further participation in any and all high school sports.

Hilton has been the pitching sensation of the state for the

past two years and the brilliance of his performances has been such that every major league club in the country has had a scout following him during the present campaign. Although big-league rules prohibit scouts from contacting and signing a high school player until after his class has been graduated, there are many loopholes in the provision. Hilton is such a prize that extreme efforts have undoubtedly been made to secure his services. The loss of the Valley Falls star . . .

Chip sank down on the side of the bed, mouth agape, amazement written all over his face. "Well, what do you know about that?" he managed.

"I know we've got to see the Rock," Soapy growled, "but fast! Hey," he said, pivoting about, "any truth to this? Anyone try to sign you to a contract?"

Chip shook his head vigorously. "What do you think? Of course not! Come on! Let's go!"

Rockwell had been as much surprised and dumfounded as Chip as he hurriedly scanned Turk's article while standing by the dresser in his room holding the paper Gardner had thrust into his hand. He handed the paper back to the friendly scout.

"This is impossible, Gardner! Chip would no more sign a big-league contract without telling me about it than, than— Why, why who ever heard of such a thing?"

"A guy by the name of Turk must have heard of such a thing," Gardner said dryly, tapping the paper.

"Maybe," Rockwell said grimly. "I'll call Chip—"

But Rockwell didn't have to call Chip. Chip and Soapy were just outside the door and, even as Rockwell was lifting the receiver, Chip was knocking on the door.

Chip sensed as soon as he entered the room that the two men had read the story. And Rockwell's first words left no doubt.

"Chip, have you seen the morning paper?"

"That's why I'm here, Coach. Soapy just showed it to me. Gee, Coach, why would anyone write a story like that? Why, there's not a word of truth in it!"

Rockwell turned to Gardner. "I knew it, Stu," he said. "I knew it!"

Gardner nodded. "I knew it, too, Rock," he said, "but this story's *dynamite!* You realize what time it is? It's eleven thirty and you're scheduled to play at two. You've got to get busy! The state committee meets at twelve and they'll bar Chip as sure as shootin'!"

Rockwell bit off his words angrily. "Over my dead body," he said grimly. "I'll have something to say about that! I'd sure like to get hold of this guy Turk!" He turned to Chip. "You know him?"

Chip shook his head. "I never heard of him, Coach."

Rockwell spun around and grabbed the telephone. "Room five-fourteen."

"Chet? Rock! Look, we're in trouble—

"You saw it? Well, then you know. Now listen! You and the team go ahead. I'll take Chip with me and check with the committee! Don't wait! Take your licks and infield workout and keep the kids on their toes! We'll be along as soon as we clear this thing up. What's that?"

"Smith!"

"But there isn't anyone else!"

"He's right here! Now get going! We'll probably be there as soon as you are. I'll clear this nonsense up in a hurry."

"O.K.! Good! Get going!"

Rockwell was all action now. He sent Soapy flying to join Stewart and then hurried away with Chip to meet the state committee. Stu Gardner had not been idle either. He had been trying to figure a way to help out. He didn't share Rockwell's confidence that the state committee could be handled so easily, and he was on the telephone before Rockwell had entered the elevator. It was unusual for a scout for one club to call another chain, but this was an emergency. Gardner liked Rockwell and he liked the Valley Falls kids. And if there was any way to clear up this mess and help Chip Hilton, Stu Gardner had made up his mind he was going to do it.

The whole thing smelled fishy to him and his voice betrayed his anxiety as he addressed the operator. "Call me back as soon as you get through, will you, please? I'll talk to anyone! It's *very* important!"

Gardner sat down heavily on the bed and tried to figure it out. The Bison management was Grade A, played the game square. Stu was sure of that. He knew the Bison main office had never authorized a scout to sign any boy before the deadline. And he knew them well enough to be sure that they would tell him if any of the Bison scouts were here. He hadn't seen Bill Peterson or Rudy Miller. They were the top men in the Bison scouting organization . . . Maybe it was someone new. . . .

Stu was still clutching the paper. He glanced at the story again. "Jimmy Turk," he muttered. "I'll call *that* bird, too! Mr. Turk's gonna have to do some fast talkin' to me!"

Gardner got immediate action on that call. "Everyone was gone for the day," a disgusted voice advised.

Where could Jimmy Turk be located? Huh! Look in the telephone directory and good-bye! Didn't he realize this was Saturday?

Gardner leafed through the telephone directory. No Jimmy Turk was listed. Then the phone rang, but it was only the operator. "Sorry, Mr. Gardner, that number doesn't answer in Chicago. Saturday, you know—"

Gardner knew it was Saturday by this time and he knew something else. Jimmy Turk would be at the game, was probably there already. Anyway, Stu Gardner was going to get going and find him. As the taxi followed the long line of cars heading for University Field, Stu was thinking about Rockwell and Chip and hoping they were making out all right with the committee.

But they weren't making out at all! A. K. Beldon and the other members of the eligibility committee couldn't agree with the frantic Valley Falls coach. "You'll just *have* to understand our position, Rockwell," Beldon was saying firmly. "In spite of what you say and much as we want to believe Hilton, here, we have no alternative but to suspend the boy until we have proof of some kind."

Rockwell was boiling. "You mean that's proof?" he demanded, pointing to the paper.

"Not necessarily," Beldon said slowly, "but it is a public statement, and has been read by thousands of people this morning who are vitally concerned with the boys and the sports of this state. We've got to take some action. We'd be erring in our responsibilities if we passed it over without some evidence to disprove the assertions." He turned to Chip.

"Did you ever talk to a Bison scout, Hilton?"

Chip shook his head. "No, sir," he said firmly, "that is, not to my knowledge."

"Did you talk to *any* scout?"

"Oh, yes, sir. Several, in fact."

"Was there an agreement of any kind? Verbal or otherwise?"

Chip shook his head vigorously. "No, sir. Never!"

"This is all nonsense!" Rockwell bellowed. "The boy has told you he never signed anything! What more do you want to know? I never heard so much nonsense in my whole life!"

Nonsense or not, Beldon and his committee members were obdurate. Despite Rockwell's arguments, they stood their ground. Chip Hilton was declared ineligible and must remain ineligible until more information was forthcoming.

"But look at the time," Rockwell said impatiently. "It's one o'clock now and the game starts in an hour. Where could we get any information in that little bit of time? That's stupid! The boy's word is as good as gold! I'd stake my life on it!"

Beldon assured Rockwell that he and his committee believed Chip, too, but that further information was imperative. Then he eased the situation somewhat by advising the worried coach that he had learned Jimmy Turk had been assigned to cover the game for his paper and that the secretary of the state association was in the press box at that very minute awaiting the sports writer's arrival.

"We'll have Turk on the phone the minute he shows up, Rockwell," Beldon continued, "and we'll try our level best to get the facts."

"Facts!" Rockwell snorted. "Huh! That's a big help!"

Beldon glanced at his watch. "It's one fifteen now, Coach," he said soothingly. "Why don't you leave Hilton with us and go on out to the game? As soon as we can get any information at all that will clear the boy we'll rush him to the field."

All the time Beldon had been talking, Rockwell had been striding back and forth across the room, muttering to himself. Now he stopped and faced Beldon, cold anger blazing from his eyes and his voice choked with emotion. "But I don't have a pitcher," he stormed, "what's the use of going out to the park?"

"I imagine your boys are as much upset as you are," Beldon said quietly. "Personally, I think your place is with them. You can't do much here."

Rockwell nodded his head vigorously. "You can say that again!" he said curtly. He deliberated for a moment and then started for the door. As he passed Chip he placed a hand on the boy's shoulder. "See it through, Chipper," he said softly, "we're all behind you."

At the door he stopped again. "We'll play the game," he said, his voice cold with repressed anger, "with or without Chip. But under protest! And I'm advising you right now, that you, the state athletic association, and Jimmy Turk, and everyone else who is mixed up in this affair, are going to rue the day you permitted some jokester to keep this kid from playing in that game today. Mark my words!" The door banged and he was gone.

There wasn't a sound in the room after Rockwell slammed the door. Everyone appeared to be in deep thought. Chip was completely demoralized. He reviewed every minute of his stay in University, starting with the arrival of the team at the hotel Tuesday evening. At no time had any scout made him a proposition or asked him to sign a contract. Sign . . . Why, the only thing he had signed had been the hotel register, his letters to his mother, and a few autographs.

Minutes later, the telephone rang and Beldon was talking to Turk. Chip could gather from the one-sided conversation that the sports writer was firm in his convictions and sure of his position. What in the world was this all about? He concentrated with all his might as Beldon talked.

"That's right! That's *just* what we want to know—"

"You saw the contract with your own eyes?"

"And the two signatures were identical?"

"Did you know the scout?"

"You mean you don't know his name?"

"Would you recognize him?"

"Didn't you attempt to verify the story?"

"Of course I understand the time element! But how about the boy? How about the ethical factors?"

"But what if you made a mistake? What if it was a joke? Or a frame-up? Think what you may have done to this boy and his team—"

"Well, you'd better be right! You have placed me and my committee and the State High School Athletic Association in a terrible position and I want you to know right now that if that story proves to be false, you and your paper are in for trouble. A whole lot of trouble!"

"I'm afraid any help you can give us now is too late—"

"All right, in the field house. Young's office will probably be best. We're leaving right now!"

When Rockwell arrived at University Field, the first person he met was Stu Gardner. Gardner searched the face of the worried coach but what he saw there killed his hopes. "No luck, eh," he said sympathetically.

"No, Stu," Rockwell said wearily, "looks bad! What a mess! You locate Turk?"

"Not yet, Rock, but I will. You go ahead with the team and I'll keep you posted. The guy's gotta show up before long. Soon as I learn anything I'll let you know. Where's the kid?"

Rockwell brought Gardner up to date on the committee's action and then hurried toward the diamond. The Big Reds were taking their fielding practice when Rockwell swung through the gate by the grandstand. The big clock on the scoreboard registered one fifty.

Hustling along, out of uniform for a Big Red ball game for the first time in his coaching career, Rockwell almost made the dugout before he was recognized. Then some keen-eyed Valley Falls rooter spotted him and he was bombarded with questions from all sides.

"Hey, Rock, wait a minute— Is it true?"

"Where's Hilton? Where's Chip?"

"Who you gonna pitch?"

"What happened?"

But Rockwell merely waved and ducked into the dugout without a word. He was oblivious to the tumult in the stands and to everything except the necessity of delaying the game as long as possible. Stewart was batting fungos for the infield warm-up, but when he saw the glances of the kids, he dropped the bat and joined Rockwell in the dugout. One keen glance was all Rockwell's loyal assistant needed, the bad news was written all over Rockwell's face.

"Everything all right?" Rockwell asked tersely.

Stewart shook his head. "Nothing's right," he lamented. "Look at 'em!"

Rockwell didn't need to look. He had felt the uncertainty which gripped the Big Reds as soon as he dropped down in the dugout and caught sight of their nervous warm-up. These kids had come a long way. Limited in number, handicapped with injuries, and shy of reserves, they had fought for every run and every out through a precarious season. And the inspiration for that fight had come from the kid they had elected their captain, Chip Hilton. They had lost easy games, and had nearly fallen apart during Chip's suspension, and Rockwell knew that without him today they might collapse completely. His keen black eyes caught the covert glances directed toward the dugout and, in spite of his desire to delay the game as long as possible, he breathed a sigh of relief when the bell clanged and they came trotting in and gathered around him in the dugout.

Every boy there was thinking the same thing, but it was Biggie Cohen who voiced the question. "Chip all right, Coach?"

Rockwell shook his head. "Not yet, kids, but he will be! They're working on it now and he'll be along just as soon as they check up on a few things."

"Chip wouldn't do anything like that!" someone asserted.

Tuffy Collins snorted. "*Wouldn't!* You mean *couldn't!* Just isn't built that way!"

"We all agree on that, Tuffy," Rockwell said softly. "Now listen! We've got to go out there and fight as we've never fought before—

"Soapy, you start! You've got to hold them until Chip gets here! The rest of you get up on your toes and stay there! Give Soapy everything you've got. We beat them before and we can do it again.

"We're first at bat and we'll hit in this order: Collins; Morris; Schwartz; Cohen; Badger; Trullo; Peters— you'll be in right, Lefty; Carey, and Smith. All right, Tuffy, start us out right! Carl, you and Soapy get out there at the end of the bleachers and throw! All right—"

Rockwell's words were drowned in the roar which greeted the umpire's announcement:

"Battery for Valley Falls: Smith, pitching; Carey, catching—

"For Salem: Parcels, pitching; Overton, catching—

"*Play ball!*"

CHAPTER 17

THE BLUE CAR

A. K. BELDON had been active in the physical education and athletic program of the state for many years, but in all that time he had never experienced a situation like this one. Beldon had known Rockwell for most of those years and respected him. And he knew the boy sitting so quietly by his side almost as well as he did his mentor. It was a strange paradox, he was thinking, that you could live with a person all your life and remain a stranger, while one little hour spent with a new acquaintance often resulted in complete understanding and trust.

Chip Hilton was known all over the state for his athletic accomplishments, and Beldon knew the boy's fine record almost by heart. But he knew much more, now, about this good-looking gray-eyed youngster. And what he knew made the duty which he had to perform all the more difficult. This boy possessed real moral courage. His behavior and attitude in the face of this unexplainable situation had been admirable, and Beldon wanted so desperately to help Chip that he was almost running when he led the little group up the steps and into the office of D. H. Young, State's director of athletics.

Stu Gardner was standing by the telephone and Jimmy Turk was sitting at a table nervously tapping his fingers. The strained silence in the office indicated that the meeting between the two had been anything but pleasant.

Beldon nodded shortly and came directly to the point. "Now, let's have the whole story, Turk."

Turk told them about meeting Swarts, about the Bison contract, and about the signatures. He described his comparison of the signature on the contract with Chip's autograph on his souvenir program and then told of his attempt to reach Rockwell and Hilton by telephone.

"I had to meet the morning deadline," he explained, "otherwise I would have had more time to round out the story."

"I'd think so," Beldon grunted. "Well, that leaves us exactly nowhere!"

"Not necessarily," Gardner interrupted. "Not if we can locate the fellow Turk talked to— By the way," he added, "my name is Gardner. Stu Gardner. I scout for the Drakes and I know just about every scout in the country. And from the description Turk gave me, the man's a faker. He doesn't stack up as anyone I ever met. I've got a call in now for Commissioner Burrows! Finally located him in New York."

Jimmy Turk was feeling more and more insecure with each passing minute. And he began to realize just how serious this matter could be if he had been fooled. Not only would he have ruined this boy's athletic career, but his own as a newsman. He had avoided Chip's eyes up to this moment but now he felt he had to know the boy's reaction. "I don't want you to think I doubt you, Hilton," he began, "but how do you explain your signature?"

"I have no explanation for the signature," Chip said calmly. "You can hardly expect me to explain something about which I know nothing. I *do* know, though, that I *never* signed a contract!"

"Signatures are easily forged," Gardner added dryly.

"Where did you meet the fellow, Turk?" Beldon asked. "Maybe they know the fellow down there at the hotel."

Turk nodded nervously. "They might," he said hopefully. "If I could talk to them—"

"That's easy enough," Gardner said curtly. "I'll call a taxi!"

Beldon checked him. "Not necessary," he said, "I'll drive you in my car. Come on, Chip, you come along too, we may need you! Doc, would you mind waiting here?"

Doc Barry nodded. "I'll be here, Beldon," he said.

Gardner elbowed Turk. "What about the game? How you going to get your story?"

Turk's eyes were hard. "It looks like this is going to be a better story. Besides," he said grimly, "I want to be in on this one to the finish!"

Just as they reached the outside steps, a tremendous roar from the stands signified some important play of the game. Instinctively their steps quickened. Chip and Gardner exchanged glances but neither spoke. The cheer could mean everything or nothing, depending upon your particular interests. Chip's heart sank and his spirit rebelled. What was the use of all this? He ought to be on the bench . . . No! He ought to be out there pitching! For a brief second he almost hated Turk; felt like lashing out and driving his fists into the writer's face. But he remembered his mother's counsel and stifled the impulse.

The trip to the hotel was futile. The man Turk described was unknown to everyone in the place. Desk clerks, bellboys, newsstand girls, and even the elevator operators declared they neither knew nor remembered a person of that description.

Beldon was discouraged. "Looks like we're whipped," he said gloomily. "I guess we might as well go back to the game and wait for the call from Burrows. I'm sorry, Chip. Personally, I'd give anything to be able to give you an O.K."

Chip said nothing. But he swallowed hard as he looked out the window of the car. There went the last hope. . . .

Not another word was spoken as Beldon started back down Main Street toward University Road. Chip was still staring out the window, thinking about the game and wondering how Soapy was making out.

Soapy wasn't making out and hadn't been making out from the start. He had been in one hole after another. But he was getting used to it. Parcels had set the Big Reds down one-two-three, in the first inning, but Soapy had walked the first batter to face him, had hit the second with a pitched ball, and loaded the bases with another walk. Only a sensational double play by Tuffy Collins and Speed Morris had pulled him out of that hole. As it was, the Sailors had scored two runs.

Then Soapy had looked at the clock and at the scoreboard, and had started to stall. Every pitch became a complete act, with Carey co-operating beautifully. Carl would walk halfway out to the mound after each pitch and Soapy would meet him. Carl would hand the ball to Soapy, slap him on the shoulder, and each would about-face and stalk slowly back to his position. Soapy would pick up the resin bag, daintily dust his fingers, and nonchalantly toss the little sack over his shoulder. Next,

Soapy would look at each of his teammates and wait for words of encouragement.

It would be Carey's turn then. He would have trouble with his mask, drop his cap on the ground, loosen the strap on his glove, find a shoelace untied, and take time to brush a stray piece of clay from the plate. Squatting, finally, he would give the sign.

Soapy would then start the "shake-off" act. Carl would call for a fast one. Soapy would shake him off. Carl would show two fingers and Soapy would ignore the call. Carl would give the sign for a knuckler and Soapy would shake his head so vigorously that his cap would fall off. Finally, Soapy and Carey would agree on a sign. In reality, signs meant nothing to Soapy. His only pitch was a straight ball, in the strike zone, when possible.

The fans and the umpires were inclined to be amused at first. But when the Sailors began to complain, the plate umpire warned Soapy and Carey several times, and finally called Rockwell into a huddle with the two boys. "You're allowed twenty seconds to put the ball in play—not forty," he advised Soapy, "and if you don't hustle up a bit, I'll start calling a ball every time you exceed the time limit. You've got to keep the ball in play!"

Soapy nodded gravely and proceeded to keep the ball in play. He threw to an occupied base at every opportunity. And he had lots of opportunities. It seemed that one or more Sailors were always on base. If the fielding and throwing of the Big Reds had not been sensational, the game would have been a farce.

In the fifth inning, with Salem leading 7 to 0, the top of the Big Red batting order came up. Collins led off and got on when Parcels issued his first pass of the game. With the hit and run on, Speed smashed a hard grasscutter between the first and second baseman for a single, and Tuffy took third.

The Valley Falls fans sensed a rally and their cheers mounted to one continuous roar. Then Red Schwartz met one of Parcels' fast ones right on the nose, lining a Texas-league single to right center field. Collins scored, Speed went to third, and Cohen was up. Parcels did just what everyone expected him to do, walking Biggie on four straight pitchouts to fill the bases and that brought Badger to the plate. Chuck kept the rally going and sent every Big Red rooter into hysterics by driving the first pitch against the left-field fence. Before the rebound was fielded and returned to the infield three more runs had scored and Badger was on third. But that was it. Parcels steadied and Trullo, Peters, and Carey were easy outs, leaving Badger stranded.

But the rally had given the Big Reds a lift and they hustled out on the field for the bottom of the fifth only three runs behind. Then Soapy uttered a few silent prayers, and resumed the stalling act.

Chip would have been thrilled if he could have seen that fifth-inning rally. But, at that very moment, he was experiencing another kind of thrill. Just as Beldon turned off on University Road, Chip caught sight of a familiar blue car. In fact, the car was proceeding in the opposite direction and was going so fast that it was almost out of sight before anything registered. Then Chip came to life with a bang. "Stop!" he shouted. "Turn around! Please! Hurry!"

Beldon was startled but he reacted perfectly, braking to a shuddering stop and executing a "Dutch turn" that left his passengers hanging on for dear life. Chip was leaning far out of the car, eyes focused far down the road. Then, just as Beldon's car roared ahead, the blue car turned right on Main Street.

Chip had lost all hope of making the game by this time. Now he had but one purpose. To get at the bottom of the mystery. But deep down in his heart he was praying for the Rock and the gang. "They've *got* to win," he muttered over and over, "got to win for the Rock!"

They were nearly to the corner now, fairly flying. "Don't lose that blue car!" Chip pleaded.

Chip's companions had been rendered speechless by the sudden action, but as the car gathered speed and raced forward, they recovered.

"Why the blue car?" Gardner yelled. "You know the driver?"

Chip shook his head. "No," he hollered, leaning back into the car, "I didn't see the driver, but I know that car and I think it's the answer!"

Chip leaned back out the window and then groaned aloud. The traffic light ahead flashed from green to yellow and then to red. Beldon saw it all right, but he didn't groan and he didn't stop. He put his weight on the horn and took the turn with screeching brakes and tires.

Gardner pointed ahead. "Turning left," he called, "second corner!"

Beldon took his share of Main Street right out of the center and cut left at the second corner. And there, half a block ahead, was the blue car.

"Slow down," Chip cautioned, "don't let them know we're following."

The car ahead pulled up to the curb and Beldon skillfully swung in behind a parked car.

"Neat," Gardner said admiringly, "*extremely* neat!"

Chip didn't say a word. He was watching the car ahead like a hawk. Two men got out, one on each side of the car, and entered the building.

Gardner pointed to the sign which extended out over the sidewalk. "Tom and Jerry's," he muttered, "*and* if I'm not mistaken, a joint! Now, what?"

"It's them, all right," Chip cried. "It's Adams and Weaver! They're in this some way. I know it! We've got to follow them! They'll recognize me, though."

"Well, they won't recognize me," Gardner said grimly. "Wait here! I'll be right back!"

Gardner had aptly described Tom and Jerry's. It *was* a joint, a veritable grease spot. A long, badly scarred, wooden lunch counter extended along one wall behind which was a shelf with the usual "dirty spoon" assortment of pasty looking pies, cakes, and puddings. Several fly-specked mirrors served as a backdrop for the unappetizing display. On the other side of the room, separated from the lunch counter by a number of small tables, several booths lined the wall. A small wall radio was blaring out an account of the championship game.

When Gardner entered, dropped down on a stool at the counter, and ordered a cup of coffee, Swarts was arguing heatedly with Adams. Gardner had recognized Adams and Weaver when he had opened the screen door as the men who had gotten out of the blue car. He heard the sportscaster give the score of the game and that distracted him for a second so he did not get a look at the third member of the party. But when he lifted the cup of coffee to his lips, and caught a glimpse of Swarts in the mirror behind the counter, he nearly choked. He gulped furiously and glanced away. If this wasn't the man Turk had described, it was his twin brother! Taking another sip of coffee, he quickly appraised the fellow and his attire. Then he waited until the sports announcer gave the score again before slipping a dime on the counter and walking out.

Adams was trying to pacify Swarts. "Shut up," he growled. "I want to listen to the game."

"The heck with the game," Swarts snarled, "I want my dough. Now!"

"Keep your shirt on," Weaver said roughly, "you'll get paid! Don't you want no bonus? Hear that score? We're in!"

"And how!" Weaver gloated. "Bottom of the seventh and Salem leadin' nine to four! We're in clover!"

"Come on, Buck," Swarts pleaded, "pay me off. I don't care about no bonus."

"Take it easy, Dutch," Adams mumbled, "I'll square you up just as soon as the game's over."

"You mean if that crazy Smith ever gets Salem out," Weaver chuckled.

"Every run those Sailors get is just that much more insurance, Peck," Adams gloated. "They got the bases loaded again. Now ain't that just too bad!"

"Yeah," Weaver chuckled, "too bad for the Rockhead and the Pretty Boy!"

"Look, Buck," Swarts urged, "my nerves are all shot."

Adams pushed him roughly. "So what!" he snarled. "I told you I'd pay you off soon as the game was over. Now go take a walk around the block."

Gardner forced himself to walk leisurely until he was safely away from the lunchroom. Then he turned on the steam. "It's the guy!" he exulted, when he reached the car. "I'm positive! It's the bird we're looking for and he's talking to those two other guys. Let's go get 'em!"

Beldon grasped the excited scout by the arm. "Hold it, Gardner," he urged. "We can't afford to make a mistake! This is a serious matter and we need the law on our side. Turk can identify him, but he'll have to be careful not to let the fellow see him. Chip, you stay here and watch! I'll call the police!"

CHAPTER 18

A NEW BALL GAME

HENRY ROCKWELL was a fighter. Friends and enemies all agreed that he never knew when he was licked. But as he sat there in the dugout in the bottom of the seventh and saw Soapy working himself into another hole, it was all the veteran coach could do to resist a groan of despair. Salem was leading 9 to 4, there was no one out, two Sailors were aboard, and Soapy had just thrown one in the dirt to make the count "three and no."

The fans really got on Soapy then. They had laughed at and with him at first only to become impatient later because of his delaying tactics. Now they finally had turned antagonistic and mean when they realized that as a pitcher Soapy had nothing on the ball but his fingerprints.

But Soapy kept trying, gamely stuck to his deliberate delivery, and took the taunts and jeers like a champion. Rockwell was suffering as much as Soapy. He was throwing every pitch with the boy and he felt the bitter sting of every barb that was being directed at the lovable redhead.

Things went from bad to worse, but Soapy kept fighting and trying. Rockwell felt a twinge of shame at his own weakness, and then his fiery aggressiveness came rushing back. He glanced along the bench before he realized that what he was doing was only wishful thinking. There just wasn't anyone on the bench. Then he called time and walked out to the mound to talk to Soapy. Cohen and Morris joined him there and Nick Trullo came trotting in from the outfield.

Rockwell patted Soapy on the shoulder. "That's all right, kid," he said affectionately, "you're doing all right! How's your arm?"

Soapy swallowed before answering. "It feels all right, Coach, but I just can't seem to find the plate. You think Chip's gonna show up?"

"I don't know about that," Rockwell said grimly, "but I do know that a Big Red team never quits! Bear down, kid, we're with you! Come on, forget the crowd! They'll be cheering before *this* game is over!"

Nick Trullo touched Rockwell on the arm. "I feel great, Coach. Honest! Maybe if Soapy and I traded positions for a couple of outs—"

Rockwell shook his head firmly. "No, Nick," he said, smiling, "you worked yesterday. I wouldn't take the chance—"

"But I'm not going anywhere in baseball, Coach. What does it matter? We want to win this one for Chip."

"I know, Nick," Rockwell said gently, "but it's no go! You get back out there in left field." He turned to Soapy. "And you stay right in there, Soapy, and keep fighting! This game isn't going to be over until the last man's out!"

"Right, Coach!" Biggie gritted. "Come on, Soapy, we'll get to 'em sooner or later!"

Soapy grinned. He was his old self again. "Better make it soon," he said, waving his glove hand toward the scoreboard. "Now, what shall I do about this baby and the three-and-no count?"

Rockwell answered that question, biting off the words aggressively. "Throw a waste ball in there and put him on! Then, you just take aim at the plate and let her fly. We'll do the rest!"

It worked. Soapy threw a wide one to fill the bases and, when the next hitter stepped to the plate, took aim and let the ball fly. The batter was late but met the ball solidly, sending a ground ball burning down the right-field base line. Biggie dove for the ball almost with the crack of the bat, made a backhand stop, rolled over, and then threw from a sitting position for the force at home. That made it one away with the bases still loaded, but Soapy wasn't worrying. He took aim, let the ball fly again, and Rockwell's double-play combo did the rest. The batter drove the ball straight at Morris. Speed came in fast, took the ball neatly, and the double play was routine, "Morris to Taylor to Cohen."

Soapy was grinning widely when he dropped down into the dugout. "I'm gettin' the hang of it now," he quipped. "All you do is aim and let her fly! Wish Chip would hurry up!"

While this was going on, Chip was talking excitedly, telling his listeners about Buck Adams and Peck Weaver and their feud with Rockwell. "They've been after Coach all year," he explained, "and when I saw Buck's blue car, I was positive they were in on this contract thing. They wanted us to lose bad! Guess they knew it meant Coach Rockwell's—" Chip bit his lip and stopped abruptly. He had almost let the cat out of the bag. . . .

"Coach Rockwell's what?" Gardner asked.

"Oh—er—that it meant so much to him." Chip answered lamely.

There was a long silence then. Chip was mentally

kicking himself for being so talkative. He looked at the dashboard longingly. It didn't seem possible that there would be a car in this day and age without a radio. He wished he knew the score.

Beldon had the same wish, but he was in a position to do something about it. He called the police and then, in spite of his hurry to get back to the car, dialed Young's office. Dr. Barry's eager voice answered and Beldon gave him the news.

"We've got 'em, Doc. Yes, the fellow who showed Turk the contract and two roughnecks from Valley Falls who have it in for Rockwell! Got 'em cornered right now in a restaurant. . . . Yes, I just called the police! The game over?"

Beldon listened anxiously. "Nine to four? I'm sure sorry to hear that. What's the inning? . . . Top of the eighth? Looks as though we'll have to do something about Rockwell's protest! This is certainly a mess! Have Rockwell meet me in the office right after the game. We'll be there as soon as we get these fellows rounded up. Only good thing about the whole matter is catching up with this fake scout. . . . How do I know he's a fake? Because I believe the boy! I'll call you back in a few minutes."

Jimmy Turk, sitting in the car, was just as deep in thought as Chip. He knew, now, that he had made a tragic mistake. This kid was too eager to find the fellow with the contract. If he had signed it the kid would be acting differently. "Now," Turk told himself, "you *are* in a jam. Wait till I get my hands on that guy! He sure took me for a ride! I fell for the whole job! Hook, line, and sinker! From what the kid says about these other two guys, it might be more than just a get-even stunt. What if it's a gambling frame-up? I'd never live that down! Especially if Salem wins and I don't see how they can lose with Hilton out of the game. Boy, if I get out of this one, I'll check, cross-check, and double-check every story I write the rest of my life!"

Turk would have been more than discouraged right then if he could have known how the game was going. Valley Falls had managed to tally another run in the top of the eighth, making the score Salem 9—Valley Falls 5. But that little ray of hope meant nothing. Soapy was already in trouble in the bottom of the eighth. And with the weak end of the Salem batting order, at that! Right at that very moment, there were Sailors on first and second, one down, and with Overton, Salem's great catcher, at bat. Fortunately, Turk wasn't to know about that until later.

"Hey!" Gardner's sudden explosion startled his companions. "Look! Look who's comin' out the door! That your scout, Turk?"

"It sure is!" Turk cried. "I'd know him a mile away! What are we going to do now? He's going in the other direction! He'll get away!"

"We've got to stop him," Gardner said fiercely. "We've got to hold him until the police get here!"

"I'll hold him!" Turk said abruptly.

Before his companions could move, the sports writer was out of the car and running after the unsuspecting Swarts.

Chip and Gardner could only watch. Turk raced down the street until he reached Swarts's side and then he whirled the surprised fellow around. There was a brief exchange of words and then Swarts suddenly lashed out and knocked Turk to the pavement. But Turk was game. He scrambled up on hands and knees and tried to grasp Swarts around the legs. But Swarts backed away and kicked Turk viciously in the face. Then he turned and ran back toward Tom and Jerry's.

Just outside the door, he broke his stride, started to enter, appeared to change his mind, and finally ran directly toward the car in which Chip and Gardner were sitting.

It had all happened so quickly that Chip sat frozen in his seat, eyes glued on the advancing figure. As Swarts came closer Chip got a good look at the fleeing man's face and something clicked in his mind. He'd seen that fellow somewhere.

Then Chip was out on the walk and in full pursuit. Swarts heard him coming and stopped, but Chip had already left his feet in a full-powered, head-on tackle, and the two bodies crashed to the walk. Chip clambered up on top of Swarts and clutched him by the throat. Then each recognized the other.

"The pen!" Chip gasped. "The autograph and the pen! Where's that paper you got me to autograph, you faker?"

Swarts's answer was a violent effort to regain his feet. Gardner put a stop to that, kneeling on Swarts's arms and shoving him back to the sidewalk. Chip took advantage of the opportunity and rammed his hand into Swarts's inside coat pocket. And there it was! The paper he had autographed so innocently!

"So!" Chip exploded. "So you wanted my autograph for your sick son! Well, I hope you're satisfied! You got me out of the game, all right, but you got yourself into a jam that will take you out of circulation for keeps!"

"I'll say he did!" a strange voice boomed. "Let him go, youngster. I'll take care of the gentleman now."

Chip looked up and was shocked to find that he was ringed by a crowd of spectators. The speaker was a policeman who promptly jerked Swarts to his feet. Beldon was there, too, examining Turk's battered face. Chip scrambled up and handed the paper to Gardner.

Stu unfolded the crumpled paper and moved between Beldon and Turk.

"So *this* is your idea of a big-league contract!" he said sarcastically, holding the paper in front of Turk's face. "By the way, your eyes ever bother you? Take a *good* look this time! You ever see a letterhead? Yes? And you know what glue is? Yes?

"Well, someone pasted a Bison letterhead on a schoolbook contract, and, I *hope*, taught *you* a lesson! Huh!"

Gardner shrugged contemptuously, turned away, and thrust the paper into Beldon's hand. "That satisfy *you?*" he demanded.

Beldon nodded. "Yes, Gardner," he said quietly, "I've been satisfied ever since Chip told me it wasn't true. Right now, all I can say is that I'm sorry it had to happen and that I had to act as I did. You can be sure I'll do everything possible to rectify the mistake and to clear Chip. But first, we've got to take care of this fellow's accomplices. Officer, they're in that restaurant!"

Beldon was wrong on that score. Adams and Weaver were in the blue car and Buck was driving swiftly back to the motel. They had heard the commotion and rushed out of Tom and Jerry's just in time to witness Chip capture Swarts. Adams had needed but one glance to warn him that something was wrong. He muttered a curse and made straight for the car, Weaver following on his heels. Adams got away from there, fast. And unnoticed. Weaver was squirming and twisting.

"That kid," he muttered angrily, "he always shows up! Now what are we gonna do?"

"First, we're gonna pack up and check out of that motel," Adams gritted. "And as soon as that game's over we're gonna collect our bets and beat it! Oughtta be over pretty soon. Turn on the radio."

"Top of the ninth now—Salem leads nine to five. Schwartz leading off for Valley Falls—the redhead has one for three so far—singled, in the Big Reds' four-run rally in the fifth. Parcels kicks—Schwartz swings—it's a long one—it's over Erickson's head—could be—*Oh! What* a catch that was, folks! Erickson caught that one right up against the fence. *Wow!*

"Well, that's one away and brings Cohen up—the big left-hander is Valley Falls' cleanup hitter—batting a thousand in this game—one for one—Parcels has walked the big boy twice so far.

"Parcels won't give Cohen anything good—that's for sure! Here it comes—it's outside—one and no. The fans don't like it—they want to see Cohen hit. Parcels kicks —Cohen swings—he hits—it's in there—it's good for *two!* Hear that roar—this Cohen's a great boy.

"Rockwell's talking to the next hitter—it's Badger— Chuck Badger—a great third baseman. This kid throws like a machine gun—has two for three so far—his three-run triple in the fifth was right up against the fence.

"Here's the pitch—it's in there for a called strike. Cohen's on second, you know—staying close to the sack —taking no chances. Parcels delivers—Badger connects —it's on the ground between Curry and Aikin—Curry tries for it—he can't get it—it's a *hit!*

"Boy, oh, boy, what a stop! Aikin went deep back of third base to get that ball—Cohen's caught between the bases—he's going back—there's the throw—it's going to be close—Cohen slides—

"Well, the big boy got back but it was close.

"So—with one gone—it's Cohen still on the keystone bag—Badger on first—and Peters up. Peters is the little southpaw who underwent an appendectomy earlier in the year—hasn't pitched since. Rockwell's a stickler for protecting a kid's arm and health—otherwise Peters or Trullo might be chucking today instead of Smith.

"Peters isn't much of a hitter—Parcels has—let's see
—yes, he's struck the little left-hander out three times
in a row. Rockwell's talking to Peters—now he's at the
plate.

"Parcels throws—here comes the pitch—Peters pivots
—*he's going to lay it down.* He *does!* Cohen and Badger
are moving—Parcels is in on the ball—Peters is away—
he's going to make it—that kid can move—how about
that?—Parcels didn't even make the throw.

"That fills the bases and now—now the tying run is
at the plate—and Parcels calls time.

"Folks *that* was one for the books—smart too—Salem,
way out in front—playing deep and expecting Valley
Falls to hit away—was crossed up.

"*This ninth-inning rally is dangerous*—the dumplings
are on the fire now—don't go away. The score again is
Salem nine, Valley Falls five—there's one away, remember, bases loaded, and the tying run is at the plate—"

Adams mouthed a curse. "Turn that thing off," he
growled angrily, "everything's goin' wrong on this deal!"

That was what Beldon was thinking, too, as he stood
there in Tom and Jerry's. Except for the man behind
the counter, the restaurant was empty and there wasn't
a sound in the place. Not a sound except the voice of
the sportscaster. Everyone stopped short and eyed the
little radio on the shelf with utter astonishment and disbelief written on his face.

"—hit a *grand-slam home run.* This is really one for
the books folks! Soapy Smith, the Valley Falls catcher,
turned pitcher for today's game because of Chip Hilton's eligibility difficulty, has just hit a *four-run home
run* to tie up the score at nine all here in the top of the
ninth. *It's a brand-new ball game!*"

CHAPTER 19

PICK-OFF PLAY

CHIP's heart leaped. "A new ball game!" Before he could control his action, his head shot around and his hopeful glance met the steady gaze of Beldon's black eyes. Beldon smiled and nodded. "And how!" he said understandingly. "Right away!"

Beldon had hoped to corral all three of the men at one fell swoop and it was difficult for him to conceal his disappointment. From what he had been able to gather, the two fellows who had escaped were the ringleaders. The man they had captured was merely the goat. But the complete vindication of Chip and the good news from University Field crowded out thoughts of everything but the game and his desire to get Chip out there as quickly as possible. He turned to the officer. "It looks as though they've gotten away, but I want to swear out warrants for their arrest. You s'pose it would be all right if I came down to headquarters right after the game?"

"If you don't mind, Mr. Beldon," Turk interrupted, "I'd like to swear out the warrants myself. I'm sure the paper will want to follow through on this, but whether it does or not, I certainly intend to do so. Besides, you're

losing time and I think Hilton ought to have a chance
to get into that game!"

"You said a mouthful!" Gardner exploded. "Get going,
you two! We'll take care of things here and those other
two birds! I know them like a book!"

Beldon and Chip were on their way without another
word. Into the car they piled, breathing excitedly, each
impatient to get to the game as soon as possible. Chip
had admired Beldon's driving skill in the chase of the
blue car, but he hadn't seen anything yet. Beldon was
hunched forward over the wheel now, eyes picking out
a path for the flying car through the afternoon traffic,
while his foot pressed the accelerator clear to the floor
board.

Later, when he recalled that wild ride, Chip remembered so many close calls that it scared him, even then.
But at the time he was conscious only that the car was
speeding him to the game. But speedy as was the trip,
events at University Field were such that it appeared
doubtful that Chip would arrive in time to see the end
of the game.

After Soapy's grand-slam homer, Parcels had been so
upset that he walked Collins. The brilliant Salem
chucker had figured Smith would be tired, had tried
too hard to strike him out, and the home run had been
the result. But with the winning run on base, Parcels
iced up and fanned Morris on three straight strikes.

Soapy took his time going out to the mound, trying
desperately to figure out a way to slow down the game.
And he was so intent upon watching for Chip that he
forgot to "take aim and let her fly" with the result that
he walked Parcels. There followed two infield outs on
two sparkling plays. The Valley Falls fans began to
hope. But then Soap fumbled Aikin's sacrifice bunt, putting runners on first and second, and promptly went to

pieces and walked the Sailor second baseman, Burns, on four straight throws.

Carl Carey rifled the ball back to the mound so hard on the umpire's "ball four" that Soapy dropped it like a hot potato. Parcels, on third, broke for the plate and only the alert recovery of the ball by Biggie Cohen forced his return and kept the game from ending right there. Then, with his teammates yelling encouragement, Soapy took aim and fired away. And he got the count to three and two on Hartman, the Sailors' long-distance hitter. But he took so long to look for the sign for the final pitch that the umpire warned him to "play ball or else!"

Carey squatted and started the usual routine with the sign for a fast one. But Soapy shook that off and continued to shake his head as Carl went right through every sign he knew and some he didn't. The umpire was so thoroughly enraged by that time that Carl called time and trotted out to the mound. What's the matter with you? What kind of a sign do you want? What do *you* want to throw?"

"Nothin'!"

"Whaddaya mean 'nothin' '?"

"I just don't want to throw nothin'! Think I'm crazy? The bases loaded, last of the ninth, three and two on the batter, and the score tied! Whaddaya mean, what do *I* wanta throw? *I* don't wanta throw nothin'! *Ever again!*"

And that was the state of affairs when Chip and Beldon came running across the field. It was one of those unforgettable baseball moments; a moment in which the spectator becomes lost in the action, is so intent and absorbed in the play that he can only wait, incapable of thought and speech, for the climax. The spell was broken when Chip was recognized and the news spread through the crowd like wildfire. In a matter of seconds one continuous roar rolled from the stands.

Beldon hurried to the chief umpire, Hooks Bolton, spoke briefly to the surprised man, and then motioned to Pat Reynolds, the Salem coach. Rockwell extended a hand to Chip and joined the little group at the plate. Then, as though by peremptory command, that great throng quieted. Every person in the park was watching Beldon and the umpire and Pat Reynolds and Henry Rockwell.

Beldon was doing the talking, reviewing the chase and the capture. Then he drew the fake contract from his pocket and handed it to Rockwell. Reynolds and the umpire crowded close to the Valley Falls mentor and craned their necks as he examined the fateful document.

The crowd in the stands must have sensed that this was the contract they had read about, for the stillness was broken as by a giant explosion. And it grew in range and volume to such an extent that a person couldn't hear the sound of his own voice even though he was shouting with all his might. Chip's teammates gathered in a little knot behind the mound and waited and hoped that this huddle meant Chip had been given a green light.

"So," Beldon concluded, "Hilton is in the clear! And he's eligible to play, Rock, if and when you want to use him."

Rockwell's glance shot toward the scoreboard and the little veins on his temples bulged under the strain of his concentration upon the decision. Then he shook his head. "No," he said bitterly, at last, "it wouldn't be fair. The boy has been humiliated and branded and tortured beyond belief for something he knew nothing about— No, it would be the greatest travesty on fair play in the history of baseball!"

"But why?" Beldon cried. "*Why?* The boy is *clear!* He *wants* to play! And you *certainly* need him."

"Not that badly!" Rockwell retorted. "Not badly enough to saddle him with the responsibility of losing a state championship with one pitch! Why, he would carry the memory as long as he lived! Nope, I'd rather lose ten championships!"

"But, Rock," Beldon pleaded, "more than the championship is at stake, now. You know how some people are! If Chip doesn't get into this game there will always be someone who will point to that fact and say he must have been guilty of *something!* This will clear him completely!"

"Beldon's got something there, Rock," Reynolds said thoughtfully. "Why don't you let the boy decide? You'll probably hurt him more by keeping him out of the game than by putting him in. Kids are funny that way, you know. They want to win, of course, but if they have to lose they like to lose as a team—like to go down together!"

Rockwell turned abruptly away, headed straight for Chip, and the crowd-noise died away as the fans followed his progress. Reaching Chip's side, Rockwell draped an arm around the boy's shoulders and shook him gently. "This is a tough spot, Chipper," he said softly, "and it's up to you to make the decision. Last of the ninth, score tied, bases loaded, two down, and the count at three and two—"

Chip didn't even realize what Rockwell was trying to say. He had been lacing his spiked shoes, hurrying to get ready. Then, as the discussion at the plate continued, he began to fear that Reynolds didn't want him to play.

"You mean it's all right with Salem if I play? Then I'm ready!"

Chip tore off his coat, stripped the tie from his shirt, and began rolling up his sleeves. "Some uniform!" he said, smiling at Rockwell.

"The uniform doesn't make the ballplayer!" Stewart said dryly.

The grim lines on Rockwell's face relaxed, and for a long moment he stood there trying to control the sudden surge of emotion which gripped his whole being. He didn't dare trust his voice until he forced himself to turn away and read the ominous figures on the scoreboard once more. That did it, and he had regained his composure when he pivoted back to Stewart.

"Give the umpire and the scorekeeper the dope, Chet. Chip's in for Lefty Peters, hitting seventh, behind Trullo. Carey goes to right field and Smith behind the plate.

"Now, Chip, the hitter is Hartman. Left fielder. Batting in the third spot. Likes 'em fast! Fouled off two of Soapy's fake roundhouse hooks. If you feel right after your warm-up, you might try something soft. But that's up to you and Soapy. Remember, the count's three and two, and everything depends upon *one* pitch. The game either ends with that one pitch and with it the loss of the championship *or* it's a new ball game!"

Chet Stewart came bustling back in time to speak out of turn and to surprise Chip and Rockwell by lapsing clear out of character. "And if we go into extra innings, Chip, Rock'll let you put on your uniform!"

That brought a smile to the lips of his listeners and the tension was broken. Rockwell waved toward the umpire and pointed to Chip. The crowd, concentrating on the scene in front of the Valley Falls dugout, caught the gesture, realized its significance, and again the din was deafening.

Chip walked swiftly out to the mound and each step

brought an increase in the crowd ovation until finally it was so great that it would have broken any sound meter in existence.

Every Big Red on the field met Chip at the mound, crowding around, pounding him on the back and the shoulders and the head and just anywhere to let him know how they felt. Chip needed a drink of water then, bad. But he felt even a bigger lump in his throat, if that was possible, a second later when Kip Parcels came trotting over from third base.

Parcels grabbed Chip's hand and pumped his arm, smiling friendly fashion, and added his good wishes. "I'm sure glad it wasn't true, Chip. Guess everyone's glad from the sound of the cheers. It's a good thing for us you didn't start! Good luck!"

Then Chip was toeing the slab, taking his warm-up throws. As he burned them in to Soapy, he realized, for the first time, how strange he must look without a uniform. But the importance of that one pitch came flooding back. ONE PITCH! Now, he knew how Soapy must have felt . . . Guess the best pitcher in the world wouldn't want to make *this* throw . . . Well . . . why make it? . . . Because there wasn't any other way. . . . Wait a minute . . . There *was* a way. . . .

On the last warm-up pitch, Soapy pegged the ball down to second and joined Chip in the alley in front of the mound. And as the umpire called, "Hilton now pitching for Smith," Chip told Soapy what he planned to do.

"But it's risky, Chip. Skip it! It's too dangerous!"

Chip's hand closed over Soapy's wrist. "Of course it's dangerous," he whispered. That's the reason it will work. They'll never expect it! You call it!"

"But why don't we tell Tuffy now—"

"Because they'll see us and get wise! Now—"

"But what if Tuffy misses the sign!"

"Tuffy won't miss it! You call it!"

Soapy trudged back to the plate, adjusted his mask, squatted, and gave the sign. Chip nodded, toed the rubber, and took his stretch. Then he lowered his hands, counted, "One—one thousand, no! Two—two thousand and throw!"

Chip's next action was so fast and so unexpected that only two persons saw the play coming. Rockwell saw it coming because he caught Collins' return sign to Soapy. But his "No! No!" was too late.

Pat Reynolds saw Aikin's big lead off second, but his warning, "Back! Back!" was never heard.

But *every* fan saw the *play*, saw the pivot and the throw to Tuffy Collins who dove for the bag and the ball and blocked Aikin a foot away from the bag for the final out of that hectic ninth inning.

CHAPTER 20

PITCHERS' DUEL

THE PICK-OFF PLAY had been as much a surprise to most of the Big Reds as it had been to Aikin. The tension of that action-packed inning had drawn each Big Red's nerves as tight as the strings of a piano and the release sent them racing for the dugout, each yelling at the top of his voice.

Chip grabbed Tuffy's hand and nearly pulled the little fighter off his feet. "Atta boy, Tuffy," he cried, "I knew you'd get Soapy's sign! What'd I tell you, Soapy? You see that stop?"

Soapy pursed his lips and shook his head. "Not me, Chip! I didn't see it! I just gave the sign and closed my eyes!"

Rockwell was as excited as anyone else. He grasped Chip's hand thankfully, and as he did so, the fans gave the boy a tremendous ovation. Chip waved his hand and ducked down into the dugout where Stewart was

holding his uniform. "Guess you can put this on now!"
Stewart said jubilantly. "What a play! What a play!"

Kip Parcels should have been tired and disheartened.
He had pitched nine long innings and his teammates
had given him a comfortable lead right up to the top of
that memorable ninth. But he didn't show it. In fact,
he seemed stronger than ever. And if his spirits had
been affected by the Big Reds' rally, he gave no evidence of it.

Chip was hustling into his uniform in a corner of the
dugout shielded by Chet Stewart and Pop Brown and
hoping that the Big Reds would have a big inning. He
wanted to get in a few warm-up throws before he went
back into the box. But Parcels had different ideas. He
set the Big Reds down one-two-three. Schwartz hit
one right back to the box, Cohen went for one across
his wrists, driving a slow roller to Burns, Salem's second sacker, and Badger topped a two-bounce grasscutter to Aikin. All three were easy outs at first. So Chip
wasn't able to get in any extra warm-up throws and had
to walk out to the mound for the bottom of the tenth
to face Hartman who had been left at the plate on the
pick-off play.

Salem's outfield was rated the best in the state for
several reasons. Hartman, O'Shea, and Erickson, batting
in that order in the third, fourth, and fifth spots, were
fast, good fielders, possessed strong throwing arms, and
they all hit the long ball. In addition, they were all portside hitters, triple trouble for a righty chucker.

Chip knew all about this trio, knew that they had
broken up a lot of ball games. It was important to get
away to a good start with the first one.

Hartman had all the earmarks of the power hitter.
The tall left fielder held his bat high, elbows away from
the body, and assumed a wide, solid stance. Chip re-

membered the two other games he had pitched to Hartman during the regular session. And he remembered that Hartman had nicked him for two solid singles, both from his fast ball. So he bent a darting hook around Hartman's belt for a called strike and then teased him with a high outside fireball. Hartman looked it over and that evened the count.

Chip came back with another hook and Hartman took a full swing, getting a piece of it, the ball clearing Smith's head and bouncing up against the grandstand for the one-and-two count. Chip was ahead now, and he shook Soapy off until he got the sign for the slider. He aimed for the center of the plate and released the ball with a high overhand delivery, swung through with his body, finishing a bit out of position but sending the darting ball past Hartman's full swing for the strike-out.

Soapy powered the ball to Biggie and the horsehide flew around the horn to Tuffy, Speed, Chuck, and back to Cohen. Biggie tossed the ball to Chip and O'Shea was up.

O'Shea was the big gun of the big three, a fixture in the cleanup spot and looked the part. The powerful center fielder was built like Cohen but on a trifle smaller scale. He walked up to the plate swinging three bats, cocky and determined. His teammates and the Salem rooters gave him a great hand and then got on Chip, yelling and jeering.

"Here goes your ball game, Hilton!"

"Bye, bye, Hilton! Kiss that ball good-bye!"

"Better walk him! Better put him on!"

Chip wasn't walking anyone, wasn't going to put the winning run on base if he could help it. He waited behind the mound, perfectly relaxed, until O'Shea tossed the two extra bats away and stepped confidently into the batter's box. O'Shea tapped the plate, lifted his bat in a high overhead stretch, assumed his stance, and glowered at Chip, arrogance expressed in his every move.

Chip took Soapy's sign and then toed the rubber. O'Shea had challenged him and Chip was determined to throw the book at the bulky hitter. Working swiftly, he poured his fast one inside, just high enough and close enough to drive O'Shea back from the plate for ball one, caught the outside corner with his slider to even the count, and went ahead with a darting hook around the knees. Next, Chip drove a blinding fast ball high outside for ball two, and then looped the blooper right smack across the center of the plate. O'Shea didn't even swing; he was still posing with war club on shoulder when the umpire called him out.

Erickson was lean and wiry, and snapped his wrists through beautifully. Chip wasn't sure but he figured Erickson might be a sucker for hooks, might at least be induced to hit them in the dirt. But he didn't curve his first pitch. He took a chance that Erickson might take one, might want to get a look at him, and he drilled his fast one right in the center of the strike zone.

Erickson watched it go by and stepped out of the box to dust his hands. Right then Chip made up his mind that Erickson had seen the last fast ball Chip Hilton was going to serve up to him that day. So Chip used his darting hook and then a teasing change-up which the skinny right fielder topped to send a high bouncing ground ball straight at Tuffy for an easy out at first, and to end the inning.

That's the way the game went, right through the bottom of the thirteenth. Parcels and Chip, matching one another in a tense pitchers' duel, continued setting the hitters down in order. The fans had quieted now, tired out by the earlier excitement and the long game, sitting on their hands for the most part, and wondering how long it would be until one of these kid chuckers would break.

The radio and television commentators had been thrilled by the action in the earlier innings, and had had plenty to describe. But now they were hard put to find something to talk about and became worried lest their audiences became bored by the long struggle. But they didn't have to be concerned about fans in Salem and Valley Falls. In those two towns there was only one program of interest to the respective citizens and they meant to sit right there by their radios until the game was over.

Adams and Weaver had no particular love for Salem, but they were two of the most rabid rooters the Sailors had for this game. After checking out of the motel, Adams had parked near by on a side road and eagerly turned on the radio.

"It was a tough spot—possibly the toughest situation any high school pitcher ever faced. But Hilton was ice water—proved to everyone who saw the play that he pitches with more than his arm. He came through the fire with one of the greatest clutch pick-off plays this observer ever saw. And now it's a new ball game—with the score all tied up at nine–nine—and Valley Falls—"

Adams, muttering curses, nearly tore the knob from the panel as he turned off the program. "That jerk!" he exploded. "That lousy show-off!"

Weaver was more worried than angry. He was worried about the bets he and Adams had placed but he was also worried about Swarts. "You think he'll squeal?" he asked abruptly.

Adams' head jerked around as though pulled by a string. His close-set eyes were mean and angry and the veins on the side of his neck were thickly corded. "You mean Swarts? Huh! He don't know nothin'!" He gestured contemptuously. "He's the one that pulled everythin'! He got the signature and showed the contract to the pencil pusher! No one's got anything on us!"

"Whaddaya think they'll do to him? What *can* they do?"

Adams reached for the radio knob again. "Nothin'!" he said shortly. "Nothin'!"

"And now it's Salem's turn at bat with the big end of the stick coming up—Hartman—O'Shea—and Erickson—"

Adams again turned the knob. "I can't stand this!" he said irritably. "I'm goin' over there on the grass and do some thinkin'. Let me know when it's over."

University had been thronged by hundreds of Valley Falls rooters that morning. A few had come up with the team earlier in the week and some had arrived Friday night. But the bulk of the Big Reds' fans had driven over that morning. No matter when they had arrived, all of them had managed to get the paper carrying the story of Chip's ineligibility.

Petey Jackson had been one of the first to hear the story and he rushed to tell John Schroeder. Schroeder had gone into a huddle with Doc Jones and worked up a plan to keep the story from reaching Mary Hilton. Schroeder had taken her to lunch and Doc had "just dropped around" to see George Morgan, owner-operator of the Valley Telephone Company, to tell him about the ugly rumor that was being circulated about Chip Hilton and to suggest that Mary Hilton be given the afternoon off.

George Morgan blinked a couple of times, mentally calculated what per cent of the outstanding telephone stock Jones and Schroeder owned, blinked again, and warmly agreed that it was "just the right thing to do!"

And that explained why Mary Hilton, John Schroeder, and Doc Jones took off on the three-hour drive to University at one o'clock that afternoon.

Mary Hilton was concerned about the time. "We'll be a little late, won't we?" she asked.

Doc Jones assured her that the championship game was always a long-drawn-out affair and if they arrived at the game around five o'clock they'd probably be in time to see the most interesting part. It was just too bad that the radio in John Schroeder's car was on the blink. Schroeder went along with Doc on that, laughing it off, but then, of course, he didn't know that Jones had pulled a whole fistful of wires out of place.

Mary Hilton had alway known John Schroeder to be a careful man, but most everybody drove faster than thirty miles per hour on an open highway. And for a man who was on the way to a ball game, she thought he made an awful lot of stops, really for no reason at all except to find out the score.

Doc always made it a point personally to dash into the garage and get the score. And if he wasn't a very accurate reporter, you'd have to admit it was all in a good cause. "The kids are way out in front!" he assured his listeners, blandly omitting to tell them that it was the Salem kids.

It was exactly six o'clock when they stopped for the last time, just outside the town of University. Something must have happened at that stop which Mary Hilton couldn't understand. For Doc Jones came flying back, puffing and wheezing, and as excited as she had ever seen anyone in her life.

"It's a *tie* game!" he shouted. "*Nine* to *nine!* Last of the *eighteenth!* And *Chip's* pitching! *Step on it!*"

For the life of her, Mary Hilton couldn't see anything

to cause all the sudden excitement. And she was further bewildered when John Schroeder snatched his hat off his head, tossed it over his shoulder, and yelled, "Yippee!"

Before Mary had gotten that figured out, they were at University Field and Schroeder and Jones each had her by a hand and were running for the gate.

Chip had never felt better in his life. He had plenty of smoke and his hook and his slider were darting streaks of lightning. And, in spite of the wind which had sprung up and was blowing briskly into his face, his control was perfect. So far, he had thirteen strike-outs to his credit.

There were two down and Erickson was at bat when Schroeder and Jones arrived, fairly dragging Mary Hilton between them. Some of the grandstand fans had gone home and there were several vacant seats directly behind home plate. Doc spotted them and led the way, snatching up a paper lying on an end seat and handing it to Mary. "Spread that on the bench," he said excitedly; "keep your suit clean!" He grabbed Schroeder by the arm. "Boy, what a game this must have been! Eighteen innings!"

Mary Hilton was still holding the paper when Chip wound up and pulled the string on his hook and he had his fourteenth strike-out. The fans gave him a big hand as he walked to the dugout and Chip lifted his cap. Then he walked to the bat rack and got his favorite stick. He was on deck behind Trullo.

Parcels was emotionally and physically tired. He had gone eighteen long, nerve-racking innings and, unfortunately, he wasn't blessed with the frame and the stamina which Chip possessed. Besides, the wind was affecting his control.

Rockwell had noted Parcels' fatigue and he urged Trullo to "look 'em over!" "He's dead tired, Nick," he said. "Wait him out!"

Trullo waited him out and it paid off. Nick worked Parcels for the full count and then walked when Kip barely missed the outside corner. Chip, batting lefty, had flied out in the eleventh, walked in the fourteenth and slashed a two-bagger against the right-field fence in the sixteenth. So, here he was in the top of the nineteenth, batting five hundred, and with a chance to win his own game. That is, if he didn't have to advance Nick.

Rockwell had been waiting for a break, but now that it was at hand, he didn't know what to do. Chip was a good hitter and Parcels had handcuffed Carey, who followed Chip, the whole game. And since Soapy's ninth-inning round-tripper, Kip had struck out the red-head three times.

Chip, on the first-base side of the plate, went through his batting ritual. Then, just before he stepped into the batter's box, he glanced at Chet Stewart in the third-base coaching box. But Chet was looking out at the scoreboard; Chip was on his own! He dug in, noted the positions of the outfielders, and took a good toe hold. At that moment Hooks Bolton, the plate umpire, called time.

Pat Reynolds walked out to the mound to talk to Parcels and Chip stepped away from the plate. He knew what that conference was all about. Reynolds was instructing Kip to put him on, give him an intentional walk. The Salem coach was matching wits with Rockwell! Chip was right. Parcels threw four straight pitchouts and Chip trotted down to first, Trullo moving to second.

Carey followed orders and tried to lay it down, but

Parcels kept the ball at the top of the strike zone and Carl popped up to the catcher for the first out. Soapy came up then, grim-faced and determined, but as tight as a drum. And his swing was just as tight. With the count at one and one, Rockwell, desperate and taking a long chance, put on the hit and run. But Soapy tried too hard, missed the ball by a foot.

Trullo and Chip were away with Kip's pitch but Nick wasn't fast enough. Overton's peg cut him down at third by ten feet. Chip overran second purposely, hoping to draw a throw, but Curry was too smart, and held the ball. That made it two away, the count on Soapy one ball and two strikes. After a close one evened the count at two-two, Parcels broke Soapy's back and his heart with a slow curve for strike three and the Big Reds' big chance was gone.

Chip warmed-up quickly and eyed the hitter advancing to the plate. It was Curry, Salem's third sacker, and Chip breathed easier. He had Curry's number. And that number was *three. Three strikes.*

Kimmel, Salem's tall first baseman, was the fourth Sailor who hit lefty. Chip had his number, too, but this time Kimmel was late on his swing and got a piece of the ball lifting a high fly back of third. Badger went back for it, but Trullo, playing toward center field, cut over for the catch and Chuck called, "Take it, Nick! It's all yours!"

Trullo was coming full speed, hustling to get under the ball. And it was this hustle that caused the trouble. He got there too soon. Poised for the catch, he brought a gasp of heartbreaking dismay from his teammates and every Valley Falls rooter in the park when he suddenly backtracked and missed the catch. The wind had caught the spinning ball and driven it back over his head.

Kimmel was playing heads-up baseball, running everything out, and he reached third just before a frantic Chuck Badger recovered the ball and burned it in to Chip, covering the bag.

Baseball victories often depend upon unpredictable events. These are called the breaks of the game. This was one of those breaks. And it went against the Big Reds.

As soon as the ball was in Chip's hands, Rockwell called time. This could mean the loss of the game. One bad play, now, one little bobble, and this game would be over. "Tough luck, Chip," he said warmly, "it's just one of those things. Don't let it get you down! Stay in there! You can pull it out!" Rockwell was stalling for time, giving the kids a chance to settle down.

Chip waved understandingly to Trullo who was shaking his head and slowly walking back to his position. Then Chip nodded grimly and answered Rockwell. "I'm all right, Coach," he said sturdily.

Reynolds called for the squeeze then, but Chip spoiled that by keeping the ball high and low and Overton fouled off two twisters before striking out on a fireball that nearly knocked Soapy off his feet. That made it two down, with the winning run on third and Parcels at bat. Chip half expected Coach Reynolds to send in a pinch hitter then, but it was Kip himself who stepped into the batter's box.

Chip cross-fired a fast one for a called strike, pulled the string on a slow twister which just missed the low outside corner, and got ahead on a slider which cut under Kip's bat for strike two. Then Chip missed the outside corner with two more hooks and it was three and two, the full count.

Once again the game hinged on one pitch. Chip took his time, and then put everything he had on his fast one.

Parcels swung wildly, barely topping the ball and sending it spinning just outside the limed third-base line. At the crack of the bat, Kimmel broke for home and Parcels sprinted to first.

Chip dashed for the ball but Badger beat him to it, stabbing desperately at the spinning sphere with his glove hand, trying to knock it away from the line. But just before his last frantic stab, the ball struck a small pebble, bobbed crazily into fair territory too late for a play at the plate or at first, and spun slowly to a stop while Badger, Soapy, and Chip stood helplessly watching. The game was over!

And the Sailors were the new baseball champions of the state!

CHAPTER 21

THE LAST STRAW

THE SALEM dressing room was a frenzy of emotional release. The Sailors were expending all of their pent-up hopes and fears in one hilarious cheer after another. They quieted for a brief moment to listen to Rockwell's congratulations and to give a cheer for Valley Falls and then they went at it all over again.

In the Valley Falls dressing room the contrast was almost unbelievable. It didn't seem possible that the quiet, almost silent room, was occupied by fifteen or twenty persons. One or two of the players had taken their showers and the faint hiss of the spraying water was the only sound that could be heard. The others, for the most part, were sitting in front of their lockers thinking, or slowly removing their uniforms. Right after the game, Rockwell had given them a little talk, blaming himself, as usual, for the defeat.

"It's all right, kids," he had said consolingly, "you were great! *I* pulled the boneheads. Let's forget about it! You can't win *all* the time! *Someone* has to lose! And since it had to be us, let's be good sports about it and take it with our heads and our chins up! O.K.?

"Right now, I want to shake hands with every single

one of you. I want to congratulate each of you for your part in playing on the best baseball team I ever coached! I'm proud to have been your coach."

Rockwell then had shaken hands with each boy, finishing up with the seniors last, warmly gripping the hands of Soapy and Biggie and Speed and Red and, at the end, with Chip. Everyone stood there, silent, and each one of the five seniors felt as if the Rock had been saying something personal just to him. The room was so quiet that the soft sound of the water in the shower room seemed like a roaring torrent. After a moment, Rockwell broke the silence.

"Well, I guess I'd better go over to the Salem dressing room and give them our congratulations. They're a great bunch and they've got a fine team. I'll be right back."

After Rockwell had left, Chip leaned back against the door of his locker, tired in body and in mind. Beside him, Nick Trullo was bent forward, elbows on knees, head supported by his hands. Nick blamed himself for losing the game. Chip didn't look, but he knew Nick wasn't sitting that way because of fatigue. The big southpaw was trying to conceal his tear-welled eyes. Chip felt awkward and uncomfortable and wondered what he could say to help this heartbroken kid. He was glad when Kip Parcels came in and walked directly to his side.

"Tough luck, Chip," Parcels said, extending his hand and helping Chip to his feet. "It was a bum break."

"The best team won, Kip," Chip said warmly. "You pitched a *great* game! You had to go the whole way too! Nice going!"

A few minutes later, Beldon and Reynolds and Rockwell came in together. They were talking about the game and every boy in the room overheard their conversation.

"It was a tough break, Rock," Reynolds was saying in his soft drawl. "Particularly so—in view of all the trouble—"

"It sure was!" Beldon added. "By the way, Rock, while I've got you two fellows together, maybe we ought to discuss the protest."

Rockwell interrupted him. "*We* have no protest!" he said quickly. "We lost fair and square! If we had been able to pitch Chip all the way it might have been a different story and again it might not—

"That's what makes baseball such a great game! The uncertainty of everything! We lost to a better team. No, I'll take that back, we lost to a *great* team! The boys and I have nothing but admiration for the new champions of the state! But watch out next year!"

Mary Hilton was still clutching the newspaper when the game ended. The first thing she had seen was Turk's story about Chip. During the last inning, while her excited companions concentrated on the play on the field, she read the story of the contract. And, through that disastrous nineteenth inning, she sat quietly thinking about the long series of difficulties that had faced her son all through the season. She knew that somehow the truth had been discovered in time for Chip to play, but she was amazed that his spirit had not been broken completely. Her pride in her tall son brought the mist into her eyes. There was so little a mother could do. . . .

Later, after that fatal last play, she assured John Schroeder and Doc Jones that she would prefer to go right home. And when Schroeder suggested that they take Chip along, she shook her head. "No," she said firmly, "Chip belongs with his teammates."

However, the ride home and the long wait until Chip finally arrived seemed an eternity to Mary Hilton. It was nearly midnight when she heard his steps on the porch. An instant later Chip's arms were around her, and he was swinging her around and around and laughing and chattering like a magpie. But he wasn't fooling his mother a bit.

Mary Hilton knew her son, knew when he was tired, disappointed, and low in spirits. And she knew he was worried now, lest she learn the story of his ineligibility. So, wise mother that she was, she beat him to the punch, made it easy for him. "I saw the game, Chip," she said, laughing merrily at his surprise. "And," she continued, "I read the story in the paper! I'm proud of you, Chip. Proud that you controlled yourself."

That was the opening Chip needed and he poured out the story, relieved that he could now get it off his chest. He told her about Adams and Weaver and the capture of Swarts. And, as Mary Hilton learned more of the details, she began to understand why John Schroeder and Doc Jones had been so insistent that she go along to the game. But she didn't tell Chip about that, just tried to comfort him and make him forget the loss of the championship.

"After all it was just a game, Chip," she said, "one of many you've been through and only one of many more you'll go through when you go to college. And you can't expect to win all the time. The other team likes to win a championship, too, once in a while."

"I know that, Mother. It isn't so much the loss of the championship. Salem's got a great team and it wasn't a disgrace to lose to a team like that. It's the Rock! And his job!"

"I wouldn't worry about that, too much, Chip. After all, Coach Rockwell has been here too many years for anything like that to happen. Why, everyone in town likes him. I wish I could tell you what all they've planned for him Monday night at the banquet but it's all supposed to be a surprise. Goodness, he could be the principal if he wanted the job."

"But he doesn't want to be the principal, Mother, he just wants to be the coach! But remember what I heard Doc Jones say? Remember what he said? That if we lost, the mayor was going to announce the Rock's retirement?"

"Yes, I remember, Chip. But I wouldn't put too much stock in it. You may be sure J. P. Ohlsen will have something to say about that! Now, you run along to bed. And sleep late tomorrow morning. We'll have a late breakfast."

But Chip couldn't sleep that night. He tossed and turned, and all night he fought the thoughts and worries which tortured his rest. In the morning, he tiptoed down the stairs and out on the porch. Sitting there on the stoop, he anxiously checked through the front and sports pages of the *Post* and the *Times*. But there was nothing about Rockwell's retirement and he breathed a sigh of relief and began reading the story of the game.

Pete Williams' story played up the "breaks of the game" and lauded Chip's pitching. He called Soapy an unsung hero and pronounced the season to be a great success. Chip was most interested in Williams' reference to the fake contract.

"Save for the regrettable, but understandable, action of the state eligibility committee, the championship might have been retained. The one bright spot with respect to the false ineligibility charge was the complete vindication of William "Chip" Hilton. It is understood that one of the perpetrators of the serious hoax is under arrest and that the police are seeking several others, two of whom are reported to be local residents."

Muddy Waters was, if nothing else, consistent. He

continued his attacks on Rockwell, maintaining that the Big Red mentor should have pitched Trullo in the first game so he could have been available for the championship game. He cited the previous year's victory and Trullo's great pitching. But the part which made Chip's blood boil and which was so unfair that the boy could scarcely restrain himself, concerned Waters' reference to Rockwell's responsibility for the eligibility difficulty.

"Rockwell is directly responsible for the loss of the state championship. . . . A coach's *first* responsibility is the boys under his supervision . . . The parents of the players expect the responsible person to *be* responsible . . . And the glaring failure of Henry Rockwell to protect his team members and particularly William Hilton, in this instance, from contact with the person or persons responsible for the incident which resulted in Hilton's suspension until the last of the ninth inning is but one more reflection upon the veteran coach's methods *and an additional recommendation for his retirement*. . . .

Chip crumpled the paper in his hands. This article would add fuel to the fire. He wished he could think of something to do.

Just before bedtime that night Chip and his mother had a long talk. Graduation from high school had been an important goal for each. To Chip because it brought him closer to the day when he could really be the head of the little home and assume its responsibilities, and to Mary Hilton because it was a big step toward her dream of a college education for her son.

"I'm proud of you, Chip," she said softly, "proud of your success in sports and your achievements in school. It doesn't seem so awfully long ago when you were no bigger than a minute and your father and I were dreaming of the day you would graduate from high school."

Chip clasped his mother in his arms, then dropped

his head to her shoulder. There was no teasing and laughing and swinging around tonight, this was a communion which comes all too seldom to mother and son. Mary Hilton held Chip tight, gripped by that demoralizing panic which comes to every mother when she realizes her boy is growing up. And Chip lost himself in the refuge every boy treasures most, the haven of peace he finds in his mother's arms.

Graduation day dawned bright and sunny, and nine o'clock found Chip and his classmates all dressed up, nervous and excited, in the auditorium for the graduation rehearsal. The boys were attired in blue coats and white flannel trousers with white shoes, while the girls wore white afternoon dresses and white pumps.

It was eleven o'clock before Zimmerman was satisfied and dismissed them with strict orders to assemble in the main gym at "one thirty! Sharp!"

Taps Browning was waiting on the broad landing outside the main entrance when the group spilled out the wide doors. He rushed to Chip's side and handed him a copy of the *Times*.

"Look at the front page, Chip," he said breathlessly. "Rockwell's been retired!"

Chip's heart sank. Biggie, Soapy, Speed, and Red crowded around him as he unfolded the paper. And there it was, just as he had feared.

COACH HENRY ROCKWELL RETIRED

Mentor Past Retirement Age
Ruling Effective July 1

Mayor Condon, ex-officio chairman of the Board of Education, announced this morning that Henry Rockwell, a member of the physical education staff and coach of the Big Red football, basketball, and baseball teams for the past thirty-seven years was being placed on the retirement list as of July 1.

Rockwell is two years past the retirement age established by the State Department of Education, and his tenure of service qualifies him for full pension benefits.

Under Rockwell's direction, the local high school athletic teams achieved considerable success. However, the application of the state retirement act makes it imperative that he be replaced.

No mention of a successor was made in the brief announcement, and since the notification was received shortly before this paper went to press, it was impossible to contact Rockwell and secure a report upon his future plans.

"I knew it!" Chip murmured. "I *knew* it!"

"The Rock didn't," Speed said bitterly, "you can bet on that!"

"Wonder where he is?" Soapy mused.

"Chet wasn't here, either," Biggie said thoughtfully. "Bet they're in the office."

"Well, let's go see," Chip suggested.

Rockwell wasn't in the office nor could Chet Stewart be found anywhere in the building. They walked out to the broad landing of the gym entrance and sat down on the steps, each boy trying to figure out what to do.

"Bet they're home! Up at Rock's house!" Soapy said suddenly. "What d'ya say?"

"I say we go!" Chip said grimly. "But I think we ought to take the present with us. Come on, it's in my locker."

"That's a good idea," Biggie agreed. "It'll give us a chance to talk to him."

"Yes," Schwartz said thoughtfully, "I guess Rock could use a little moral support, right now."

"That's what's wrong with this picture," Speed muttered. "How come Ohlsen and Stanton and Thomas let the mayor and his crowd get away with it?"

"Ohlsen didn't know it," Chip said abruptly. "He was out of town! He's coming back special for the banquet tonight!"

"Well, how about Stanton and Thomas?" Schwartz asked.

"They were outnumbered," Chip explained. "You see, the mayor had Davis and Greer and Cantwell all lined up against Rockwell and when Ohlsen was called out of town on business, why—" Chip checked himself, but it was too late.

"Hey," Soapy said sharply, "you been holding out on us! You know something! Come on! Give!"

Chip had no recourse then, so he told his buddies everything except the part the loss of the championship game had played in the action against Rockwell. It was a sober group of youngsters who stood on the Rockwell porch a few minutes later. Chip was clutching the little package and trying desperately to figure out what he was going to say, but his mind wouldn't function. He was in a fog.

Soapy had been right. Rockwell was at home and Chet Stewart and a stranger were with him. Mrs. Rockwell smiled graciously as she ushered the five boys into the living room. "Here's some more visitors, Hank," she said. "Suppose you introduce your guest."

Rockwell gestured toward the boys. "This *is* a coincidence, Dave," he said, "here're the very guys we were talking about—

"Boys, this is Dave Young. He's down here to talk tonight at the banquet, as you know. Mr. Young is the director of athletics at State, and since you're all going to be up there this fall, he's a good man to know. Dave, this is Soapy Smith, Biggie Cohen, Red Schwartz, Speed

Morris, and Chip Hilton. Chip was the captain of the ball club."

The boys shook hands with Young and then stood there awkwardly shifting from one foot to the other.

Chip broke the silence. "I—we wanted to see you, Coach, before graduation and before the banquet tonight to—to give you a little present from just the five of us—"

Soapy tried to help out. "You see, Coach, we're all seniors and we won't be playing for Valley Falls any more and—"

Rockwell laughed. "I know *exactly* how you feel," he said. "It looks as though we're all in the same boat." He nodded toward the paper on the table. "I guess you've seen the *Times*. You see, Soapy, I won't be coaching Valley Falls any more, either."

A few minutes later the five boys were on their way to the Sugar Bowl. They were silent for a while, each feeling that the little expedition had somehow missed the boat.

"Speed's right," Cohen said slowly, "something's wrong!"

"Yeah," Schwartz agreed, "something *sure* is wrong."

"Maybe he's gonna run for mayor!" Soapy suggested.

"That's silly!" Schwartz said disgustedly. "The Rock doesn't want to do anything except coach! Don't be a dope!"

Cohen summed up every boy's thoughts. "It's a dirty deal," he said glumly, "but you know the Rock! He's tough! He wouldn't let *anyone* know how he feels!"

It was nearly one o'clock before they reached the Sugar Bowl and by that time the news was on the lips of everyone in town. The story caused almost as much confusion as the senior administration day. The older folks were resentful and openly critical. Practically everyone, with the exception of a small group headed by Jerry Davis, was sorry to learn the bad news.

At one o'clock the *Post* came out with an early edition. It should have been called the "Rockwell Special." Practically the entire front page and all the sports page was devoted to the retirement story and to Rockwell's achievements. His thirty-seven-year record in every sport was shown in one column, and the list of championships the Big Reds had won under his direction down through the years was listed in another. Smack in the middle of the page was his picture. Chip felt a glow of happiness as he read the double-column story. At least the *Post* was standing by the Rock.

COACH HENRY ROCKWELL TO RETIRE

VETERAN MENTOR'S LAST YEAR
Announcement Made Today

The Valley Falls Board of Education announced today that Coach Henry Rockwell would retire from his duties at Valley Falls High School on July 1. The veteran strategist is completing his thirty-seventh year of service.

During the thirty-seven years Coach Rockwell has been at the helm of the Valley Falls athletic program, the Big Reds have dominated the southern part of the state in football, basketball, and baseball. Rockwell's teams have won twenty-two of thirty-seven section championships in football, nineteen in basketball, and fourteen in baseball. In All-State competition, the Big Reds forces have won more titles than any other contestant.

Rockwell's success has not been limited to victories, championships, and titles. His personal interest, unswerving confidence, and loyalty to each boy who has played for him has built up in this community a love and respect which is a far greater tribute to the man than the hundreds of cups, trophies, medals, and plaques which are on display in the Big Reds' trophy room.

There was much more to the story, but by this time Soapy had consumed his fourth sandwich, second piece of pie, his third malted, and was ready for action. "Let's go!" he said. "Let's do something!"

"What?" Speed queried. "Just what?"

Soapy had twenty answers for that question. They wouldn't show up for graduation. They'd detour the banquet. They'd picket Mayor Condon's office. They'd get up a petition. They'd burn Condon in effigy. They'd burn the whole Board of Education in effigy— That is everybody except Ohlsen and Stanton and Thomas. They'd— Well, wasn't that enough?

While that tirade was pouring from Soapy's lips, Chip had been trying to figure out some course of action, but nothing seemed to make sense. He finally decided that the best thing was to see the most powerful man in town. "Tomorrow," he announced decisively, "we'll go see J. P. Ohlsen and find out if *he* can't do something about this! Right now, we'd better get a move on or we'll be late for the exercises."

"Who cares?" Soapy demanded. "Graduation ain't gonna be no fun, now— Nor the banquet, neither!" he concluded glumly.

An hour later the Valley Falls High School graduating class was seated on the stage in the auditorium. Chip felt foolish sitting there, with people looking at him and at his classmates as if they were on display in a store window. But a moment later he located his mother in the audience of proud relatives and, from way up there, far as it was, he could see the pride shining in her eyes. Suddenly he was filled with such a glow of thankfulness that the weight in his chest almost choked off his breath.

Chip didn't hear much of the graduation address, because he was thinking back through the four short years he had been in Valley Falls High School, and he felt almost like a fellow must feel when he loses all his friends. He looked at his mother again and he resolved that he'd get through college if it was the last thing he ever did and he'd come out with an education, too! Come out equipped to do something worth while. . . .

Four years weren't so long. Why, if he worked hard, those years would fly just like the past four years. And then he'd be sitting up on the stage, if they sat up on a stage when they were graduated from college, and his mother would be sitting in the audience looking just as beautiful and as proud as she looked today. . . .

Then Chip saw Mr. and Mrs. Cohen, and Mr. and Mrs. Morris, and Mr. and Mrs. Smith, and Red Schwartz's father and mother, and he got to wondering if Biggie and Red and Speed and Soapy and he would all graduate from college together. Anyway, they had all decided to start out together. In September. Up at State. . . .

Just then, the speaker sat down, and there was a great burst of applause. So Chip joined in, too. He tried to remember what the man had said, but all he could recall was something about the warmth that a fellow should feel for his teachers and the loyalty he should give to his ideals. Chip looked around for Rockwell, then, but he wasn't there.

A little later Chip heard Biggie's name and then his own name and he got up and followed the girl in front of him until he reached Zimmerman and took the long, white cylinder which said forever and forever that he was a high school graduate and that he was ready for college.

Then he was standing in front of his seat and he heard "Smith" and he watched Soapy walk slowly up to Zimmerman. He half expected Soapy to come out with some kind of a wisecrack until he saw Soapy's face.

Soapy's face was all set and determined and intense and then Chip saw the redhead looking down to where Mr. and Mrs. Smith sat in the third row. And when Soapy made the turn at the end of the stage and walked back to his seat he was still looking that way. And right then, for the first time, Chip realized that everyone took Soapy too much for granted, they didn't really know him.

Chip got to thinking, then, about the game and how hard it was to lose. He thought about Kip Parcels and, for the life of him, he couldn't help thinking that Parcels was genuinely glad he had gotten out of that hole in the ninth inning. That Kip had been glad that everything had been squared up at the top of the tenth so they could fight it out on even terms. And Chip was happy that if he had to lose to anyone, it had been to a swell fellow like Kip. . . .

That foul twister had sure caused a lot of trouble. If only he had been able to reach that ball when it was outside the line, when it was spinning so crazily around in foul territory. . . .

Yes, that little twisting ball which had lit foul and then squirmed fair had hurt. Had cost him the game, and the Big Reds the tournament, and Valley Falls High the championship, and had probably been the last straw which cost the Rock his job. . . .

CHAPTER 22

"WE'LL KILL 'EM!"

MOST sports dinners are lively and happy occasions,
often boisterous in their celebration of a successful season or a championship. But the great throng of youngsters and adults who jammed every inch of space in the
banquet hall of the Valley Hotel were strangely subdued. And although the appetizer and the steak and
the ice cream and cake were delicious, there were many
persons seated at the closely crowded tables who were
merely toying with their food.

Doc Jones, one of Valley Falls' most popular citizens,
was a good toastmaster with a salty sense of humor.
But he quickly sensed the futility of trying to rouse the
spirits of this throng. Consequently, he hurried things
along, cutting short his announcements and introductions, substituting speed and action for levity. It was a
relieved toastmaster who finally arrived at the climax
of the affair: to the presentation of J. P. Ohlsen who was
to introduce Henry Rockwell, "Hank" to the older folk
of Valley Falls, and "Rock" to every sports-loving en-
thusiast.

Ohlsen made no effort to speak, but turned and
grasped Rockwell's hand and then led him to the center

206

of the table where two microphones flanked the state runner-up trophy. The two men stood there with clasped hands, facing the throng of sports-minded friends who rose to their feet and cheered. This ovation came from the heart as an expression of love and admiration which could never have been adequately put into words.

When the applause died down a bit, Ohlsen followed Doc Jones's example and made his introduction brief. Raising Rockwell's hand in the air, he said simply, "Our coach!"

Once again cheers and applause rang out from every corner of the room until Ohlsen raised his hands. Then, after a time, the demonstration reluctantly died away, and finally everyone was seated and it was quiet.

Ohlsen waited a moment and then waved his hand dramatically toward the big plate-glass windows which faced Main Street. "You can pull those curtains now," he said.

Everyone turned to look, and there, right up on the sidewalk, spotlighted so perfectly that it had the appearance of being on the inside instead of the outside of the window, was a brand-new, shiny Buick. And up on the hood was a sign "FOR THE ROCK."

There was another cheer and a storm of applause which was almost deafening. Rockwell stood looking down at the table and two little muscles stood out on each side of his tightly clamped jaw.

"And, Hank," Ohlsen continued when he could make himself heard again, "here's the title to the car, and here's a certificate entitling you to a thousand gallons of gasoline. And here's an envelope and I think you'll like what it contains—a few promises by Uncle Sam amounting to thirty-five hundred dollars— Government bonds!"

"This last envelope, Hank, contains your retirement and pension papers and I'm sure everyone will be glad to know that it calls for a monthly payment of—"

Rockwell's outstretched hand checked him. "Excuse me, J. P." he said softly. "I, I— May I say something now?"

Ohlsen nodded. "Why—why, of course, Hank," he said heartily, "of course. Go right ahead—"

Everyone was looking at Rockwell now, noting his erect carriage, sun-tanned face, and alert black eyes. And many were thinking that despite his age and years of experience, the Rock seemed right in his prime.

Chip was one of those. He know the tireless physical energy of his coach, the lightning-like alertness of his mind, and how much he loved his work. "It isn't right," he muttered, "it isn't right—"

After a brief pause, Rockwell began to speak. His voice sounded a bit shaky at first, but after a few words, it came clear and strong.

"I hardly know where to begin, but I suppose I ought to start with the car." He smiled ruefully. "Speed Morris and I have been struggling along with a couple of antiques for a long time. Anyway, it's swell and it's too much. But I appreciate the generosity and I promise to drive it carefully. The bonds will help a lot and, well, what more can a fellow say about that—"

There was a swell of laughter, and when it ceased, Rockwell's face sobered as he continued. "Louise and I have felt, and will always feel, that Valley Falls is our home. We have seen our two boys grow up, go through grade and high school here, and then go on to college and to careers in other parts of the country. And we know that any success they may have attained or will attain was due to the training and inspiration they obtained from the people and schools of Valley Falls.

None of us will ever forget the many friendships we have made in this fine town and which we cherish with all our hearts.

"I will never forget the ups and downs our teams have encountered, the thrills of the successes and the heartaches of the defeats—

"The trophy room and its evidences of great deeds fills my heart with pride and the friendship of all the fine boys who have played for Valley Falls, and for me, is the greatest treasure I have.

"Now, I suppose I must say something about the retirement pension. I believe a pension means a person is being retired because he has reached an age where there is question about his usefulness in his job. I cannot accept that premise and I cannot accept the pension.

"So, good friends, neighbors and athletes, for everything else, I thank you from the bottom of my heart."

There was no applause, only a silence which was a greater tribute than the cheers had been. Rockwell sat down in his chair between Ohlsen and the guest speaker and the thoughts which ran through the minds of the people in that room carried back through the years. And there was sadness in the hearts of most of them and shame in the hearts of some.

Chip was having a tough time controlling the lump in his throat, and although he succeeded in that effort, he still couldn't keep his eyes from misting a bit. His thoughts were flying back through the years he had played for the Rock . . . His broken leg . . . The championships he had helped to win . . . The championship ball the Rock and the team had given him that year he had had to sit on the bench . . .

Then Chip thought about the pension and looked back at Rockwell. "It's his pride," he muttered, "he's always had pride. Lots of it!"

And when Rockwell had finished speaking and sat down, the five seniors at the honor table suddenly were aware for the first time what this graduation banquet really meant. This was good-bye . . . Good-bye to the Big Reds . . . And to Ohlsen Field . . . And to the *Yellow Jacket* . . . And to Prof Rogers and Old Pop and Principal Zimmerman and Chet Stewart . . . And all their pals . . . And, most of all, good-bye to the Rock. . . .

No more tongue-lashings when they were deserved and no more pats on the back when they had them coming. And no more private meetings with the Rock up there in the little athletic office where a fellow could speak right out and say how he felt and be sure his problem, and anything he said, would be welcomed by the man with those friendly black eyes and that twisted smile of understanding. . . .

Chip cleared his throat and shifted in his chair and four other boys seated at that graduation table did the same thing. And then, as from a long way off, they heard J. P. Ohlsen introducing the guest speaker.

D. H. Young, Director of Athletics and Professor of Physical Education at the State University, was a regular traveler on the banquet circuit. He was extremely popular with the sports fans of the state and much in demand as an after-dinner speaker. Young considered attendance at these affairs important to his work, and accepted as many invitations as possible. He had welcomed this invitation for several reasons, the most important being his treasured friendship with Henry Rockwell. And his speech reflected the warmth and feeling in his heart. Chip didn't hear much of the first part of the guest speaker's talk, but toward the last he heard every word.

"Statistics show that one boy in sixteen hundred with

a high school education achieves something really notable in life. But one out of every seventy-two boys with a college education—*one out of seventy-two boys with a college education*—leaves his mark on the world!

"And since I have learned that a great number of the boys and girls of this graduating class are planning to attend the university next September and—in particular, five members of the state runner-up baseball team— I feel I should warn you that—

"As the representative of your university and mine, I am authorized to proudly announce the appointment of Coach Henry Rockwell to the athletic staff of State University as head coach of freshman football, basketball, and baseball—"

It took several seconds for the words to register. Then you would have thought a giant bombshell had exploded in the room; there was a roar which threatened to break every piece of glass in the room. And it grew and grew until every person was on his feet and they were all cheering and shouting.

Chip didn't know just how it came about, but somehow he was on his feet, too. As he stood there yelling and cheering with the rest of that happy throng, his heart was jumping and his thoughts were racing . . . This must be a dream . . . He was hearing things . . . No . . .

"Coach Rockwell has sent us some of our greatest athletes and while he was coaching here at Valley Falls we were content to let him stay. But now that he has been retired, we can take him to State where we've wanted him for the past twenty years!"

It had to be true because everyone else was cheering and applauding and the Rock was looking straight at him and smiling and nodding his head. . . . It *was* true! . . .

They'd all be together again . . . All of them . . .
Biggie and Soapy and Red and Speed and . . . And
the Rock and him . . . At State! . . .

Then, just as they had clasped hands so many times
in so many tense moments on the football field, and on
the court, in the dressing room, and before the baseball
games during the past four years, and just as if they had
rehearsed it a thousand times for this special moment,
the five boys around that honor table joined hands. And
then their eyes shot toward the Rock and they all had
the same thought and they whispered almost in unison:
"We'll kill 'em! We'll kill 'em!"